PICTURE
FOREVER

—PEAK VALLEY FOREVER SERIES—

AMANDA LEE DIXON

Picture Forever

Amanda Lee Dixon

Copyright © 2020 by Amanda Lee Dixon

All Rights Reserved

Cover design by MaryDes
Website: www.marydes.eu

Editing Services by Silvia Curry
Website: www.silviasreading.webs.com

Amanda Lee Dixon

Table of Contents

Prologue

I thought working part time for my brother Eric as a private investigator would be fun. Full of adventure, car chases, maybe a fight or two, but so far, it's been a lot of waiting and watching.

Eric has me watching a house Sheriff Warren McKnight thinks some drug dealers are operating out of. Normally, I would pass on a job like this, but Eric's fiancée is pregnant and getting close to her due date, and he isn't too keen on leaving her side for long stints. At least the money is good and since my brewery isn't up and running yet, income is kind of a must.

Supposedly, this two-bit drug dealer moved to Peak Valley a few months ago and is trying to build an empire. Sheriff McKnight is building a case but needs more evidence before he can make an arrest. Thus, I watch the house and track what I see, snap pictures of people who come and go, along with their license plates.

It's boring, but easy money. Besides, who am I to complain? It isn't like I have much to do these days. My brothers are busy with their own lives—building families, having kids, and living that happily ever after dream. All I have is a brewery, which is still in its infancy.

"I need a life." I sit up to stretch out my back when a dark-colored van pulls into the driveway. "Look alive, Jax," I say to myself, because after sitting here for hours with no one to talk to, I have resorted to talking to myself. I pick up my cell phone, ready to jump out and snap pictures, but the way the van turns into the driveway, skidding hard to a stop, my gut tells me something is about to go down.

Swiping at the lock screen, I wait to get out of the car and call Eric.

"Bored already?" Eric answers the phone.

"A van just arrived. Two males wearing dark clothing just jumped out, and they look pissed, but they are opening the van doors like they plan to haul something large. My gut says something big is about to go down," I share, watching the two males as they pound on the front door.

"I'll call Warren. Can you get the plates?" Eric asks.

"Not from here, but I can take a closer look when they go inside," I offer, looking up and down the street to see if anyone would notice my departure from the car.

"No, stay where you are," Eric orders, but I ignore him and exit the car the moment the two males disappear into the house.

"I'll be quick," I whisper and slip out of the car, skirting around the dim streetlight and sticking to the shadows.

"Do not engage," Eric hisses.

"I've got this, don't worry," I whisper, then hang up on Eric's protests and switch off the volume on my phone. He always took his big brother duties way too seriously. He is always trying to protect me, but I haven't needed protecting for a long fucking time.

I mean, how hard is it to sneak up to a parked car and snap a few pictures? The streets are empty, and the neighborhood is quiet. I tap my phone's camera on and start snapping pictures of the van when I hear shouting from inside the house. From the sounds of things, these were two unwanted guests. I better hurry and get the plates before anyone can spot me.

Moving quickly, I slip around the back of the van and crouch to take a picture of the plates. Of course, they're covered in dirt, despite the van being clean. These guys aren't stupid, and if I wipe the dirt off, they'll know something's up. I'm not about to jeopardize a police case, so I turn on my flash and snap a few pictures, praying no one sees the flashes of light.

Right as I stand to leave, the front door flies open, slamming against the house with a loud bang. I'm surrounded by darkness, but I'm not invisible. My heart races as I slip into the shadows at the side of the house, moving as quickly as I can without alerting the two males who are yelling obscenities. I barely make it to the back of the house before they make it to the van, slamming the door and peeling out of the driveway.

Sticking my head around the side to check if I'm in the clear, a light turns on just over my head.

"We can't hold on to this load, Silas! What the fuck were you thinking?" a guy shouts and I pause my getaway.

"They offered half its worth!" another guy yells in frustration. "Them damn sons of bitches think they can pay me less than it's worth! Fucking assholes. I'll show them."

"We need to clear out of here. You pissed them off, and they don't play by no rules. They'll snitch to the cops… you know they will."

"They aren't going to snitch. Just shut your trap and let me handle the business," the man responds with less bite in his voice.

"You don't know that!"

"Oh, yes, I do. I took out their other supplier. They've got no one else to turn to. Once they find out Lucky is dead, they'll come crawling back to me, begging for my load, and I'm going to fucking make them beg on their damn knees, then charge them double."

A rock tumbles across the driveway toward me and I scan the darkness, making out a figure heading in my direction.

"Eric said you like to go rogue. What was your plan? Run in guns blazing?" Sherriff Warren McKnight says softly through the darkness.

I put my finger to my lips to quiet him, then point to the window directly above us. McKnight has his gun out when he comes to stand next to me, but the men in the house move into another room, shutting the light off and no other sounds can be heard until a TV blares to life.

"Any drug dealers die recently?" I whisper to McKnight.

"One was shot dead in his apartment in River Bend." McKnight shakes his head. "Why?"

"One of the guys in the house admitted to taking out a competitor. The drugs are in the house now, but they expect the buyers to return when they learn some guy named Lucky is dead."

"That won't take long. We need to get in there now." McKnight straightens and peeks into the window. "Only two guys?"

"Two were in the house when the buyers showed up. Several went in, but I didn't see if they all came out. Though, the two wouldn't have been openly talking about murdering their competitors and charging double if any of the buyers were still in there."

"Agreed," McKnight says, then pulls his phone out and makes a call. When no one answers, he swears under his breath before scanning me head to toe. "Do you have a gun?"

I narrow my eyes at him. "Yes."

"Good, we're going in."

"The two of us? No backup?" I arch a brow at him.

"Is that going to be a problem?"

"No. I'm pretty sure you and I can handle the two, but you aren't a 'guns blazing, blurring the line of law' kind of guy."

"If what you heard was true, we can lock these assholes up and throw away the key," McKnight says, pocketing his phone as I pull out my gun.

"Still doesn't answer my question," I point out. "Is this personal?"

"Personal? No. Why does it matter?"

"I'm about to run into a drug dealer's den with no backup… I want to know if I'm following you in because you have some vendetta toward these guys."

"No vendetta. They're moving into my town, wanting to pollute it with drugs and violence. We've had two teens overdose on the shit they're cooking up. These guys are a weed that, if allowed to take root, will suffocate Peak Valley, and I don't intend to sit back and watch that happen. I'm done being patient."

"Fair enough."

"Look, I called in backup, but a semi turned over just off the highway. Most of my men are working it."

Pressing my lips together, I glance through the window. "So, what's the plan?"

"We'll go in from the back, pin them in the front room, and hope like hell they don't pull any weapons on us."

"Ambush... got it." I nod and follow McKnight to the backdoor, which he silently opens while I watch through the window. When he enters, he waves me in, holding the door before slowly shutting it without making a noise.

We creep toward the front of the house, and it stinks of chemicals, burning my eyes. It's filthy, littered with trash we have to navigate around, but luckily, the TV volume is so loud it drowns the creaks in the worn floor as we approach.

We travel down a long hallway to the front living room. It's an advantage, but it also pins us between two narrow walls. If these guys pull a gun on us, it wouldn't be hard to hit us, even with bad aim.

McKnight signals to stop a few feet before the hallway opens into the front living room. With simple hand signals, he tells me to cover his back before he swiftly swings his gun around the corner yells, "Put your hands up!"

I can't see the two men where I stand at McKnight's back, and it makes me uneasy.

"I said, put your hands up!" McKnight bellows louder. "Now!"

"Okay, okay!" a guy shouts back, and McKnight nods for me to follow him as he moves into the living room.

"You!" McKnight points his gun at the younger-looking one. He's barely a man, for Christ's sake. "Lay down on the ground and put your hands behind your head."

He does as McKnight says, but the other man doesn't move, smiling at McKnight with a predator stare.

"Jax, cuff this one." McKnight hands me a pair of cuffs, keeping his gun trained on the smiling man. "Now you. Lay down and put your hands behind your head."

"Or what?" the man challenges as I kneel to put the cuffs on the man's partner.

"Silas, fucking shut up," his partner grumbles as I slap the cuffs on his wrists.

"Don't make it worse for yourself. Lay down!" McKnight growls, taking a step closer to the man.

"No," Silas taunts.

"Lay down," McKnight says with a chilling tension that freezes the room. No one in the room moves; collectively, we may all be holding our breath.

"Are you going to make me?" Silas whispers, letting his hands drop.

"Get your hands up and lay down," McKnight says through clenched teeth, taking a step closer.

"Silas…" his partner hisses, laying cuffed at my feet as I train my gun on Silas.

"I've got your back," I tell McKnight, and he takes another step closer.

"Are you going to shoot me?" Turning his question into a dare, Silas shifts his gaze to me and winks.

"Last chance," McKnight says, close enough to haul Silas off the ratty couch. Silas tilts his head back and laughs before reaching into the side of the couch, pulling a gun. His movements are fast, but not fast enough for McKnight, who lunges for Silas, pinning his arm and holding the gun against the couch. Silas bucks against McKnight's weight then knees McKnight hard, and he drops to a knee. The hold he had on Silas' arm loosens and Silas raises it, shooting McKnight.

Blood splatters across Silas' face as the bullet slices through McKnight's shoulder.

Before I can move to help McKnight, he brings his gun up and shoots Silas, who laughs as the bullet hits his chest and he drops the gun, still laughing as blood soaks through his shirt.

McKnight kicks the gun my way and backs up, holding a shaking gun trained on Silas.

"You're dead. Both of you. *Dead*," Silas wheezes out in a strangled laugh as McKnight radios in for an ambulance.

And this was supposed to be a boring gig…

Picture Forever

1

~ Hazel ~

"Warren?" I rush into my brother's hospital room before coming to an abrupt stop. I knew he would be surrounded by medical equipment, attached to an IV, but I wasn't expecting to see Warren McKnight Sr., my brother's father. He isn't my father—a blessing I send to the good Lord every time I encounter the stoic, imposing man with the stone-cold stare. Our mother remarried a much nicer man and had me not long after.

"What is *she* doing here?" Warren Sr. narrows his eyes, scanning me from head to toe with obvious disdain. He never liked me—I served as a reminder that Mom had moved on and he didn't.

I've barely spoken half a dozen words to the man. Though, if I had spoken more to him, he never would have acknowledged them. Warren Sr. is a narcist with expectations so high, he himself can never reach them… but don't tell him that. He'll deny his inadequacies and point out your own. I've never met a man more talented at making others feel small, especially my brother.

"She's my sister, Dad. Back off," Warren groans from the hospital bed.

With a sneer, he puts his hands on his hips, sizing me up. "I thought you lived in Kansas City."

"I… I moved back." I blink, surprised I was able to speak at all. He's the former sheriff of Peak Valley—a man who made it his mission to uphold the law—but his cold, calculating demeanor has always given me the chills. He's never displayed an ounce of kindness over the years I've had the unfortunate pleasure of being in his presence. Everyone in Peak Valley holds their breath when he walks by. Mom used to tell me to never engage, keep my distance, and never, *ever* get in trouble with the law.

"Was that your idea?" Warren Sr. asks my brother, but it sounds more like an accusation. It wasn't Warren's idea; in fact, he thought I was being too dramatic by coming home.

"Why does it matter?" Warren bites back, shifting in his bed with a wince. The familiar tension he carries in his shoulders whenever his father is around must be straining the gunshot wound he just received.

I used to fear Warren was being abused, but Warren Sr. never laid a hand on him. He's just a cold, emotionless man, and thankfully, my brother is the complete opposite. Warren can be distant and come across as cold, but deep down, he has a kind heart and a deep-seated need to ensure everyone is safe.

"I see." Warren Sr. rubs his jaw, pinning me with a stare. "I'll be by later to check on you."

"Don't bother." Warren frowns. "I'm getting out of here soon."

Warren Sr. eyes my brother for a moment before turning on his heels and leaving the room without a passing glance.

"Don't be scared of him," Warren says as he rubs his shoulder.

"The room seems warmer now that he's gone." I try to smile and move to stand by his bedside. "He hates me."

"He hates everyone." Warren shrugs, pulling me into a stiff hug. Warren isn't a hugger, and a moment passes before I return it. *Maybe getting shot made him take a hard look at his life?* "Don't let him get to you."

Easier said than done. Warren Sr. made it difficult for Warren and me to have a relationship growing up. All I ever wanted was to hang out with my big brother, but Warren thought it best that we kept our distance in public. I resented Warren Sr., but as I got older, that resentment turned toward my brother. I began to believe he was embarrassed to be seen with me, and that idea took its toll on me. I couldn't figure out what was so wrong with me that he wouldn't want to be around me. I felt like I was Warren's dirty little secret, and for most of my teen years, self-doubt crippled me. It wasn't until I left for college did Warren really start to reach out, but the damage was already done, and I kept my distance.

"What are you doing here?" Warren asks with a grunt as he reaches for the cup of water at his side.

"Really?" I raise a brow at him. "You were *shot*. You have a hole in your shoulder and currently residing in a hospital. Did you really think I wouldn't come see you?"

"You didn't tell Mom, did you?"

"No." I sigh, taking a seat at the foot of his bed. "I didn't want her to get upset."

"Good." Warren nods. "How is she doing?"

"Come visit and see her for yourself." I twist his toe, but not enough to hurt him.

"Don't start." Warren pulls his foot away with a brief smile. "I'll come see her soon. I've been busy ridding this town of drug dealers."

"Such a hero," I huff, pretending it isn't a big deal what he does, but it is. I admire him for his service—he's dedicated to Peak Valley and his deputies. I just wish he could show Mom and me just a little bit of that dedication. "She still has her memory, but it won't last forever. Try to make some time for her before it's too late."

"Don't lecture me, Hazel," Warren warns. "I agreed to Sunday dinners, didn't I?"

"I didn't come here to start a fight. I wanted to make sure you were okay." I hold my hands up. Since the move, we have tiptoed around Mom and her failing memory. Neither of us has accepted her Alzheimer's diagnosis.

"I'm fine. I'll be better once I get out of here." Warren shifts, his face grim with the pain he's trying to hide. He looks out of place in a hospital bed, vulnerable. I've only seen my brother vulnerable once, and that was when he learned the love of his life, Lily James, left town without saying goodbye.

"Are you taking the medicine the doctors are giving you?" I question, knowing my big brother will tough out the pain, even if it's against the doctor's orders. He's tough as nails, wrapping himself in armor that makes getting anything through his thick skull impossible.

"Yes, Hazel," Warren grumbles. "You sound like Mom."

I smile at him and laugh. "Thank you. I have achieved my goal."

Warren rolls eyes but smiles, and I feel the divide between us shrink just a little bit. "How are you settling in?"

"Good. The movers delivered everything two days ago. I managed to get everything unpacked in a few hours. I don't know what that says about me, but when you get healed up, maybe you can help me hang some of the art I brought back?"

"Sure." Warren nods, smiling at me like he always does when I start to ramble. Growing up, Warren and I may not have had a close relationship—and now that we are older its superficial at best—but deep down in the dark recesses of my heart, I hope moving back to Peak Valley will help bridge the gap between us. And moments like these give me hope.

"Can I get you anything? Food? Comfortable jammies?" I ask, reaching for something to keep the conversation going.

"Jammies?" He frowns and I roll my head back and laugh. He joins in my laughter, and it warms my chest. "I'm fine. I don't need anything. Do not bring me *jammies*."

"Are you sure? You'll be more comfortable." I wink.

"I'll be more comfortable once I get out of here."

"Okay…" I nod, my smile fading. I'm out of things to talk about and that warmness in my chest turns into a blanket of disappointment. "I guess I should let you rest…" I stand from the bed.

"I'll come by this Sunday. The three of us can have dinner together." Warren must have sensed my unease; he's too good at reading people, but I appreciate his attempt to make things better all the same.

"Mom would like that. So would I." I nod and wave at him before walking away.

My move back to Peak Valley was primarily so I could spend more time with Mom before her Alzheimer's steals her away from me. The doctors said early to moderate stages can progress quickly—two to four years. Moderate to late stages takes longer to progress, but there is no telling what she will be like. It was a blow I didn't see coming, and it left me feeling alone and empty.

I left Peak Valley to attend college where I received a bachelor's degree in graphic design. I started an internship at a graphic design firm the summer after I graduated and never left. I loved my job. I loved the people I worked with, but I dreamed of starting my own business and being my own boss. Only one problem with that dream… I'm not a risk taker. For years I planned the launch of *Hazel Wood Designs*, never thinking I would actually strike it out on my own… that was until my mom told me she was diagnosed with Alzheimer's.

The next day I set everything into motion, too emotionally stunned to let self-doubt and fear change my mind. I wanted to be close to my mom, and I needed a job to support myself. It was a logical decision.

As I get close to the hospital exit, I look down and dig into my purse for my keys, only to smash into someone. A bag falls to the floor with a loud thud that echoes down the hall and contents spill out around our feet.

"I am so sorry," I say to the pretty woman with bright green eyes who frowns at her bag… or more like her life if her purse is anything like mine, spilled out for everyone to see.

"No, I'm sorry. I should have been watching where I was going," she says, kneeling to pick everything up.

"Same." I kneel and pick up a notebook that's fallen open to scribblings of flower arrangements and color choices. "Are you getting married?"

"Maybe," she huffs, rolling her eyes. "I mean yes." She waves off with a hand. "But no one will *know* that since my photographer broke her foot and can't take my wedding pictures."

"Your photographer?" I ask, closing the book and handing it to her as we stand.

"I *know* it isn't her fault. I'm just a little stressed and when I'm stressed, I have a tendency to overreact." She laughs at herself. "Know any photographers willing to capture my happy moment at the last minute?"

Yes, me!

"Yes, I do." I smile at her and then dig into my purse, looking for my freshly printed business cards. "Me."

"No way." The pretty green-eyed woman places her hand on my forearm. "Either you're joking with me or I'm the luckiest person in the world."

"You and I both must be the luckiest people in the world." I giggle and hand her my business card. "I'm a graphic designer, but I have done several photoshoots. I promise I'm experienced and know how to take beautiful photos. I'm Hazel Wood, by the way."

"Amber Baker, soon to be Amber Colson." Amber takes the card and looks down at it as if it's a gift from the big man upstairs. "Hazel Wood Designs. I *love* it."

"Thank you."

"Are you new to Peak Valley? I never heard of you," Amber asks, looking up at me with nothing but kindness in her eyes.

"I'm not exactly new to Peak Valley, but I did just move back home. I decided to start my own business. Full transparency, you'll be my first client… and my first wedding, if you do choose to book me. But I promise I know what I'm doing. Check out my site." I point at the business card. "I have my portfolio up for you to see my work."

"I have a good feeling about this. I think it was meant to be." Amber smiles, pointing my business card at me. "I like you. I'll give you a call, but I've got to get to work, otherwise I would chat more with you."

"No problem. I look forward to hearing from you." I smile at her and wave as we go our separate ways. My heart swells with hope as I walk to my car, and I look around the empty parking lot before doing a little happy dance.

Picture Forever

2

~ Jax ~

"I don't understand why she couldn't let me take her photos. You've seen my pictures," Burns grumbles at my side as we sip on a beer, watching the guests arrive for Luke and Amber's wedding reception. Amber wanted to get the photos out of the way while the guests arrived, and only the couple has gone missing—apparently too impatient to get to the wedding night festivities.

"No one wants Polaroid pictures as wedding photos, old man." I chuckle and pat his shoulder. It was only a few months ago that he dug out his old Polaroid camera and started taking pictures and now all of a sudden, he's a professional.

"I would have used my *phone*, jackwagon." Burns glares, shrugging off my hand. "I got the one with the fancy camera features."

"The way your hands shake, they'd all be out of focus." I point at his hands with a teasing smile. "You schedule that doctor's appointment yet?"

"I'm old, Jax, I don't need a doctor to tell me *that*." Burns exaggerates his eye roll. *Deflecting as usual.* Over the last few months, since returning to Peak Valley, I've had the privilege of staying with Burns and Miss Janet until I was able to move into my older brother Clint's apartment. I saw the slow decline in Burn's health during those few months. It was something I wasn't prepared for, but at least Miss Janet has been an ally, taking him to appointments, making sure he takes his medication, and not letting him overwork himself.

"Where are Amber and Luke?" my brother Eric asks as he and his fiancée Sarah make their way over to where Burns and I snagged prime spots close to the bar.

"Hopefully they're too busy getting *busy* to remember we have to take pictures," Sarah says with a laugh, clutching her pregnant belly and taking a seat at the bar. "I feel as big as a whale, and the last thing I want is for it to be memorialized in my sister's wedding photos."

"You look beautiful." Eric kisses her temple while signaling the bartender for a beer.

"Drinking when your woman can't?" Burns arches a brow at Eric. Always stirring up drama, the man gets a kick out of making us squirm.

"Where's Luke?" Clint asks when he sees us. He's carrying his giant two-month-old son Axel, who is wearing a shirt with a tux printed on it. Clint is best described as a quiet giant. He's the tallest and the thickest out of all of us Colson brothers, and his son is going to be his mirror image if he keeps growing like he has.

"Stop being impatient." Dawn, his wife, rolls her eyes and takes Axel from him. She's a petite woman and standing next to Clint, she looks almost pocket-sized. I still can't believe Axel came out of such a tiny woman. "They'll get here when they get here. Besides, it's their day. They have to right to keep us waiting."

"Luke likes to be fashionably late. It's his M.O.," I say, lifting my beer to my lips, but I pause when a pretty blonde with a camera walks into the reception hall with a bright smile. It's a smile that lights up a room, but it's her innocent, wide-eyed look that captures my attention. She's wearing a light blue sundress—one appropriate for church and not flirty like the other single ladies at the wedding are wearing. She's understated, nice yet not too noticeable, but I noticed her. She's familiar, but I can't place her, and I doubt she's ever been on the receiving end of my charm. She isn't my type, but my interest is piqued.

She looks over at me, and her smile widens as if it's just for me and saunters my way. "Who's that?" I whisper to Burns.

"Who?" Burns looks around, his attention landing on the beautiful blonde. "The photographer?"

"She's off limits, Jax," Eric warns quietly before she gets close to where we are all standing. I raise a confused brow at him, and he only shakes his head.

"Hi," she greets, looking at us all. Her brown eyes are like melted chocolate with an excited glint. "Where's the happy couple?"

"Late." I flash her a full watt smile and adjust my tie, ready to lay on the charm.

"Oh." She frowns and looks over her shoulder. "Hmm."

"Can I get you a drink?" I ask, signaling to the bartender.

"No, thank you. I'm working," she says and turns on her heels, walking away, leaving me with my mouth hanging open.

"I told you she's off limits," Eric says, holding back a laugh as I watch the woman leave the reception hall. I'm not used to being shot down so quickly. Most women come on to me.

"Why? She seeing someone?"

"I don't know." Eric shrugs into his beer. "But even if she isn't, she's off limits."

"Who is she?"

"The photographer," Burns answers, looking at me like I'm an idiot.

"I *know* she's the photographer." I didn't know that, but the camera around her neck makes sense. "What's her name?" I exhale on an exasperated breath, only to perk up when she walks back into the reception hall, racing toward us.

"I found Luke and Amber. Can you all come with me? Outside?" The woman waves for us to follow. "I promise to get all the pictures taken before the food is served. Come on."

"Let's move, I'm starving." Sarah stands from the barstool and once again, the beautiful photographer turns on her heels and heads for the door, my family following and still, I don't know her name.

*****

I've been watching Hazel since she pulled us outside for wedding photos. I heard Amber say her name, but it didn't clue me in on the familiarity. It's a puzzle that I can't figure out, so I watch her, learning as much about her as I can, picking up little details about her. She's happy, and I'm becoming a stalker. Her smiles are dazzling behind the camera, and I wish she wouldn't hide it so much. It's a beautiful smile that is contagious.

I've tried to get close to her, talk to her, but she's gone before I can get more than a couple words out. It's driving me crazy. I can't tell if she's too preoccupied capturing moments to memorialize or playing hard to get. I'm going to have to get crafty if I want a chance to speak with her. This game she unwittingly is playing intrigues me.

"Uncle Jax, will you dance with me?" My niece Emily tugs on my hand, and an idea formulates in my head. She was the flower girl in the wedding. Her dress matches Dawn and Sarah's light blue bridesmaids' dress, only puffier, designed for a young girl, and she's been twirling around ever since Grandma Linda helped her put it on. Her adorable twirling has been a popular moment Hazel has taken many shots of, and I plan to capitalize on it.

Thankful for my adorable little niece, I smile down at her. "Say the magic words and you've got yourself a dance partner."

"You're my *favorite* uncle." She smiles widely at me, bouncing on her toes.

"Let's boogie." I tap her nose and take her hand, leading her to the dance floor close to where Hazel is taking photos of Amber and Luke dancing.

I twirl a giggling Emily around and around until she gets dizzy, and I pick her up before she falls over, keeping track of Hazel as she slowly gets closer to us.

"She's a cutie," Hazel says behind the lens of her camera not two feet away.

"She is, isn't she." I smile at Emily, who smiles back. "Did you know I'm her *favorite* uncle?"

"Did you bribe her?" Hazel fires back with a wink. And there's my in. Now it's my turn to lay on the charm.

"Nope. Right, Emily?"

"Nope," Emily repeats. "Take our picture!"

"You got it, cutie." Hazel laughs and it's music to my ears. I never knew a laugh could be so attractive, and I wonder what other sounds I could coax out of her. "Say cheese."

"Cheese!" Emily squeals with a goofy smile that looks more like a grimace than a smile.

"This is a great picture. Want to see?" Hazel asks, looking at her camera display, then turns it to show Emily and me.

Emily studies the picture. "I like it."

I step closer to Hazel to see the display better and breathe her in, and she's smells like sweet summer nights. "It is a good picture," I say as I study the photo of Emily squeezing me in a tight hug with her big, toothless grin.

"It's all Emily." Hazel laughs, running a finger down Emily's cheek.

"Do we know each other?" I ask, feeling confident.

"Yes," Hazel says, pulling the camera out of sight. "Excuse me. I need to get back to work."

Before I can say more, she's gone, scanning the room for more picture opportunities, once again leaving me standing with my mouth open.

What the hell just happened?

"I want down." Emily pulls my attention from Hazel.

"Sure, munchkin. Go play and remember, I'm your *favorite* uncle." I put her down and she runs away from me without a backward glance. It seems I have that tendency with women.

I make my way back to the bar where McKnight is sitting with his arm in a sling, looking bored. Not that long ago he and my brother Eric were mortal enemies… okay, they basically couldn't tolerate each other. Until they had to bring down a scammer stealing thousands of dollars from residents at the Peak Valley Retirement Community. Joining forces made them tight, and now they spend a lot of time together as friends, which at first was weird. He was enemy number one for most of my childhood, and on the receiving end of many of my pranks.

"How's the shoulder?" I ask as I signal the bartender for a beer and take a seat next to McKnight.

"It's healing up nicely." McKnight shrugs over a glass of amber liquid.

"And the asshole who shot you?" I side-eye him, pulling my wallet out and dropping some cash onto the bar.

"Pleaded not-guilty and wasn't let go on bail. He and his partner will go away for a very long time. We have too much evidence against them," McKnight shares, turning in his seat, his watchful eyes scanning the reception hall.

"Will I have to testify?" I take the beer the bartender hands me and turn in my seat, looking for Hazel.

"Probably. You heard him say he killed a rival," McKnight says to my disappointment. I've had enough of the courtroom after spending a better part of a week last spring listening to Amber's ex try to convince the jury he was innocent.

"And Silas' threats? Should I be on high alert?"

"Nah, he's all talk, no bite... besides, he doesn't have any friends," McKnight says nonchalantly. "I don't get a lot of threats with Peak Valley being a small town and all, but the ones I've received are all empty threats. You aren't worried, are you, Jax?"

"No, but I have received a few threats, and none of them were empty. I want to make sure I'm watching my back if I need to," I say with narrowed eyes. A threat, empty or not, should always be taken seriously, something you would think McKnight would understand.

"Sounds like you have lived a dangerous life, Jax. Any of that danger plan on finding its way to Peak Valley?" McKnight questions while adjusting his sling. He knows how to spin a conversation as good as Eric does, and it's infuriating.

"I lived a life of adventure, *not* danger, but trouble has found its way to me on occasion."

"That isn't reassuring." McKnight shakes his head with a laugh, sensing my agitation and aiming for a lighter mood. Like Eric, he can read people well—another infuriating quality.

"Hey, do you know anything about the photographer?" I ask, aiming for a safer topic. Eric and McKnight may have patched things up between themselves, but it didn't extend to me. Our friendship has been a level above tolerable, and mostly because we are complete opposites. He likes order and I'm a 'fly by the seat of my pants' kind of guy.

"Hazel?" McKnight says her name with a surprise note in his voice as he shifts in his seat and scans my face with a frown.

"Yeah, Hazel. She says she knows me, but I can't place it." I shift my eyes back to where Hazel is taking pictures of Amber and Luke talking with a few guests.

"Yeah, I know her, Jax, and she isn't your type." McKnight cracks his neck impatiently.

"How would you know my type?" I demand, ignoring the frosty stare McKnight has aimed at me.

McKnight grits his teeth. "Just trust me, she's not your type."

"Why is everyone telling me to back off of her?"

McKnight knocks back the rest of his drink, then growls, "Because she's my sister. That's why."

Well, fuck.

3

~ Hazel ~

It's funny how your mind works. One second you think you are in control of your thoughts, then the next, you're falling down a rabbit hole of thoughts. Like images of Jax in a form-fitting suit popping into my head at random. He grew a beard since high school. I was never into beards, but I like it on him. He's bigger, his shoulders are broader, but that playfulness he carried in his eyes is still there. His blue eyes are dangerous; they make me wonder what adventure and excitement I can get caught up in with him.

I crushed on him in high school—all the girls did. But I'm not in high school anymore, and guys like Jax don't make good adult boyfriends. No matter how sweet he is with his niece and nephew. Being the photographer at his brother's wedding made it easy to watch him, and I wasn't oblivious to him watching me.

Being sweet comes naturally to Jax, as natural as his good looks. He's two years older than I am, and even though Peak Valley High was small, he never knew who I was. I was the shy art student who hid myself away, watching from afar. He was quick to make others laugh and stirred up mischief. Most people saw a class clown, but I saw a knight in shining armor. Jax stuck up for the little guy, not by stepping in and taking a punch, but by defusing the situation. It was pure magic.

When it comes to Jax, you fall into two categories. You either love him or you're annoyed by him. If you loved him, it meant he stood up for you or was kind to you. If you were annoyed by him, it usually meant he pulled some kind of prank on you. I definitely fell into the 'love him' category, even though we never spoke a word to each other. Not until he failed to remember me at Amber's wedding.

I shouldn't be hurt by that. We never were in any classes together or even ran in the same circles, but my pride stings just a little bit.

I'm also not exactly his type. He prefers the scandalously-dressed women who can handle more than a vanilla-style night in bed. I'm not sure what it takes not to be vanilla in bed, but the way his playful blue eyes scanned me from head to toe at the wedding, I was willing to try until I came to my senses and realized just one taste isn't my style.

Jax likes to play the field; he isn't the settling down kind of guy, and I'm a settling down kind of gal. Why taste forbidden fruit when you know you'll crave it and can't have it?

Stop obsessing! I shake my head, clearing all thoughts of Jax, and climb out of my car and walk into my mom's small, assisted living apartment, the smell smoke hitting me hard and making me gag.

"Mom?" I call from the front door, the hallway to the living area clear of smoke. I go farther in, and the smoke scent grows stronger. "Mom!"

"Hazel? Is that you?" My mom hollers from the back patio as I enter the living room.

"Do you have something in the oven?" I call out, making a beeline to the kitchen. "Something's burning." I put my purse and the grocery bag full of salad makings on the counter and open the oven door. A wave of smoke blooms out, burning my eyes.

"Oh dear. I forgot about the pork loin," my mom says as she enters the living room from the back patio.

"It… it's okay, Mom," I choke out over the smoke, trying not to breath it in.

"I've ruined our dinner." Mom's shoulders slump as the fire alarm goes off.

"It's okay, Mom. Dinner isn't ruined. I'll call Warren and have him bring over a pizza. You like pizza, right?" I yell over the annoying loud beeps and pull the burned lump of meat from the oven and place it in the sink. I walk out of the kitchen to the patio door and breathe in deeply.

"It's not okay," Mom says, wrapping her arms around her narrow waist, devastation marring her face.

"Sit down, Mom. It's okay." I pull the screen closed, the fire alarm still beeping, and I give her a reassuring smile. "These things happen. I burn dinner all the time."

"I hate this," she says, finally moving away from where she stands and sits in her recliner.

I flip on the ceiling fan, the smoke casting a soft haze to the small, open-concept apartment. Grabbing a kitchen towel, I fan it under the fire alarm on the ceiling until it stops beeping and put the towel back. Sunday dinners with my mom have been eventful, but this one tops them all. I grab my purse and fish out my cell phone to call Warren, praying he doesn't ignore me.

"I already told you I was coming to Sunday dinner, you don't have to call and remind me," Warren answers after one ring.

"Can you pick up a couple of pizzas before you head over?" I ask, ignoring his comment. I did send him a few text reminders and a calendar invite to his phone.

"I thought Mom was cooking pork loin," Warren says.

"Change of plans. Can you pick up the pizzas or not?"

"Calm down, Hazy, I'll get the pizzas," Warren says to my annoyance. I hate when he calls me Hazy, and he knows it.

"Thank you, *War-war*. See you soon." I sigh and hang up before he can complain about the nickname I lovingly dub him when he uses Hazy.

"Warren is going to be *so* upset. He loves my pork loin," Mom mutters, rocking in her recliner while staring at nothing. Since her diagnosis, she has taken the news of her Alzheimer's with a positive attitude… until moments like this happen. They've been rare, but the more she has them, the more I fear her positivity will fade. I don't want to lose my mom this way.

She lost her husband—my father—five years ago to a heart attack. It was so hard for her to adjust from being with the love of her life to being alone. I lived hours away in Kansas City at the time, and Warren was working crazy hours, trying to grow his career. I almost moved back, but she managed to pick herself up. She was able to find happiness remembering the good times she had with my father. Now the memories that got her through the loss will slowly leave her, and I worry she will fade away as quickly as her memories do.

"It'll be okay. I'm just glad nothing happened to you." I squeeze her shoulder. "I don't want you to let this get to you."

My mom grabs my hand on her shoulder. "Promise me you won't let me become a burden."

"Mom, you could never be a burden." I move to kneel before her. "Don't talk like that."

"Hazel, we need to stop tip-toeing around my disease. My mind is going and while I have clarity, we need to make plans." The seriousness of the conversation brings fresh tears to her eyes.

"I know, Mom, and we will, but we don't have to make those plans tonight. Let's just have a meal together. One last meal where we can pretend that everything is okay. Can we do that?" I ask, not ready to face my mom's future.

"Yes, Hazel. One last meal." She cradles my face with a smile. "Only if you make me a promise."

"Anything, Mom. I'll promise you anything." I lean into her hand, fighting back my tears.

"I love you, Hazel, but you deserve to be loved, too. Promise me you will try to find happiness with a man so I can have some peace, knowing you won't be alone when my mind fades and I forget…" She doesn't finish the sentence and my heart breaks a little with what is left unsaid.

"I… I promise." I say the words, not really thinking about what she's asking of me. I only know I want to give my mom whatever she asks.

"I would love nothing more than to see you get married. Watch Warren walk you down the aisle. Your dad watching from above." My mom smiles at me, her tears slowly sliding down her beautiful, wrinkled face. "You've always been a shy girl; I don't want you to be alone. Promise me you'll try to put yourself out there."

"I promise, Mom. I'll try to find the kind of love you and Daddy had." I swallow as an image of Jax Colson in a tux with a light blue bow tie comes to mind. Only, he is the last person I would try to find love with. He doesn't even remember me. Chasing after Jax is like chasing after the wind. No, if I'm going to find love, I can't pursue high school crushes.

4

~ Jax ~

With my brother Luke's help, I've transformed *Benny's Bar* into a modern-meets-rusty brewery. *Colson Brewery* will be small—most of the floor space is consumed by brewery equipment—but there will be some space for people to come in and enjoy stonefire pizza. After I get up and running, and money starts to flow in, I plan to expand and have some outdoor seating to accommodate more customers.

I've placed an order for fifteen barrel tanks that will sit behind glass, on display for the customers who come to dine. Next to the glass enclosure is the stonefire pizza oven, nestled behind the prep table, where artisan pizzas will be created. I learned how to make pizza from a reformed criminal named Zion, who served most of his young adult years in prison. I met him while tending bar and learning how to brew beer in Colorado. Zion was the head cook in the bar, my greatest critic and a friend. When I asked if he thought I should offer pizza in my brewery, he told me to perfect my crust. 'Toppings could come from the greatest places in the world, but if you don't have a good crust, you won't have customers craving pizza. You'll just be another pizzeria with a gimmick.'

Colson Brewery isn't going to be a gimmick. I worked with my sister-in-law Dawn, and together, with what I learned from Zion and what she learned from her mother, we perfected the dough recipe before we worked on the topping recipes. Each pizza can stand all on its own, but several crusts pair well with my hand-crafted beer.

Looking around the empty customer seating area, I mentally shrug. Luke hasn't finished designing the seating and he's running behind. The wedding consumed more of his time, but I'm not worried. I have a lot of work I need to get done that takes priority over the seating, like getting the barrels installed so I can start production and figuring out my logo and branding. Everything has come together nicely, except the branding, which is becoming a source of anxiety for me. Every graphic artist I've worked with has given me branding ideas that don't align with my vision for *Colson Brewery*.

I don't think I'm asking for too much. I want a logo for the brewery and pizzeria, and separate logos and graphics for all the beers. The graphic artists have provided separate logos but there was no cohesiveness between the brewery and the beer. If I were a customer, I would have a hard time tying the two together.

I have ignored the need to look into more graphic artists for two days. I've always procrastinated tasks that frustrate me, but today I am determined to do something about it. I will place at least one call, but I need coffee before I can tackle the impossible.

Sugar n' Sweet is the only café and bakery in Peak Valley, but lack of competition doesn't stop the owner from creating delicious treats and better coffee than I can ever make at home. I may be a wiz at brewing beer, but I can't brew a cup of coffee worth drinking. Luckily for me, *Sugar n' Sweet* café is only a few blocks away from my apartment.

The café has a collection of white, weathered, wrought iron patio furniture and antiques with doilies covering every available surface. It isn't like the modern cafés that are all the rage, but quaint and unassuming. It's walking into the heart of Peak Valley, witnessing the charm and the warmth this old town prides itself on.

Well, isn't this just perfect.

Hazel is sitting alone in the middle of *Sugar n' Sweet*, smiling over a cup of coffee. I'd call it fate if I believed in it. A beautiful woman like Hazel shouldn't be sitting alone. It's a sin no single man like myself should allow.

She can't avoid me when it's just her and me sitting in the middle of a café. I'll coax a conversation out of her and figure out how I know her and why she wants to avoid me. Does she know avoiding me only intrigues me, and

McKnight and Eric shouldn't have ever made her forbidden fruit.

Thankfully, she doesn't notice me when I enter the café, and the excited look she gives me when I sit down is promising... until it fades almost instantly. *That stings.* I don't normally make people frown unless they're on the receiving end of one of my pranks.

"What are you doing here, Jax?" She frowns. McKnight had to have spread some scandalous rumors about me. Why else would she brush me off the moment I sat down? I'm sure we have never met. Her familiarity has to come from knowing her brother. I would have remembered encountering her. Her bright smile is a crystal-clear image in my head, and not something I will forget any time soon.

"I couldn't just let you sit here alone. It's a crime somewhere, I'm sure." I smile my panty-dropping smile at her.

Her brows furrow deeper with annoyance. "I'm not here alone... Well, I mean, I *am,* but only because they aren't here yet. They're late... Okay, a lot late. What I mean is, I'm waiting for someone," she rambles animatedly as she glances between me and the door.

My smile widens at her long-winded explanation—it's adorable. She's definitely unlike any woman I've been with.

"And here I am." I hold out my arms and scan over her sundress and sun-kissed skin. Glossy, honey-colored hair frames her face, the sunlight giving her a halo that only amplifies her innocence and turns her into a golden goddess. What kind of bastard would leave this beautiful woman waiting? She's a dream come true, even when she frowns at me.

"Not *you*. Peter Landers," she shares, leaning forward with narrowed eyes and crossing her arms on the table. She now gives me a line of sight down her dress, and nothing is going to tear me away from that view. She has tan lines and I want to see more of those lines.

"Peter Landers… I know that guy." I scratch my bearded chin, not taking my eyes off the crease of skin nestled between two perfectly sized breasts. "He went to Peak Valley High. Is that how I know you?"

"Maybe." She presses her lips together, looking eerily similar to her brother when he's being stubborn.

"Hazel?" a man asks, coming up to our table with an unhappy frown. It's been years since

I last saw Peter Landers, but not so many that I don't recognize him. We never ran in the same circles back in the day, but I don't recall ever having any bad blood between us.

"Peter, hi." Hazel smiles at him as a blush flushes her face.

"It seems I'm interrupting you two." Peter points a passive-aggressive finger at the two of us.

"No, Jax just sat down," Hazel scrambles to explain, shooting me a glare.

"We were just catching up." I wink and sit back, getting comfortable. I'm sure Peter isn't a bad guy. Probably the kind of guy a woman like Hazel would gush to her mom about, but I called dibs on Hazel and I'm not about to sit back and let another man take what I want. Especially one who kept her waiting.

"I see." Peter presses his lips together, not buying it. I cock my head at him. His annoyance isn't directed at me—where it belongs—but aimed at Hazel. .

"Jax was just leaving." Hazel lays a hand on Peter's forearm and squeezes.

"I was?" I smile when Hazel shoots me another glare. "Why were you late?"

"Excuse me?" Peter blinks.

"Why were you late?"

Peter turns his attention to Hazel, ignoring my question. "You know I was surprised to get a call from you, Hazel." He tugs on his shirt collar. "I almost didn't come because I thought you might be like all the other women who call, but I thought I would give you the benefit of the doubt given our history together, but now I see that you're just like the others."

"Just like the others?" She jerks her head back.

"You heard about my inheritance and suddenly, you're *interested* in me again," Peter accuses, looking hurt and angry. "You come back into town, unemployed, and think hey, Peter is rich… maybe I can make him my job?"

"I'm not unemployed, and I don't know anything about your inheritance," Hazel defends herself and takes a step back. "And I don't want to make *you* my job. I thought I would see how you were doing and catch up."

"Easily said now that you know," Peter sniffs.

"Peter, you should be careful with the words you use," I warn when he opens his mouth to say more. The accusations he is throwing at Hazel are going too far, even if it is to my benefit.

"Whatever." Peter glares at me before turning his attention to Hazel. "It was… *nice* seeing you."

Hazel nods with a stunned look on her face as he turns and leaves without so much as a glance back. She slowly lowers herself into her chair. "What just happened?"

"I think you got to see the real Peter Landers. Who knew he was such an asshole," I say, forcing myself not to smile too big at my good fortune. "Now that he's gone, let's have some coffee."

"After that little stunt you pulled, *no* thank you," Hazel mutters, glancing around the café, probably trying to determine if anyone witnessed Peter's accusations. It's only a matter of time before the whole town hears about it. I should reassure her, but if the whole town thinks she's a gold-digger, then my chances just increased. Does that make me an asshole or an opportunist?

"Oh, come on. He was rude, and you heard what he said to you." I raise a hand toward the door. "The way he jumped to conclusions… it would have never worked out."

"Or you ruined what could have been the best thing to ever happen to me," Hazel counters, slumping her shoulders.

"I guess we'll never know." I pick up a lunch menu and scan over the offerings. "You hungry?"

"No." Hazel rolls her eyes at me right as her stomach growls. "I have to get back to work."

"Do you really have to work or are you trying to avoid me?" I call her out. Clearly, she's single and willing to date, otherwise why would she invite Peter Landers out for coffee? So, what is it about me she doesn't like?

Surprised, she blinks before letting out a defeated breath. "Both."

Oh, I didn't expect honesty. "Both?"

"Yes, both," she says impatiently, leaning back against her chair. "Jax, I would never be able to keep up with you. You're… too *adventurous*." The way she says adventurous makes me wonder if that is a polite way of saying I'm a playboy.

"I don't think you know me well enough to make that decision." I scratch the back of my neck, though she isn't far from the truth.

"I know you are a nice guy, but when it comes to… relationships, I think we want two different things. Now, I'm sorry but I must get back to work."

"Have another wedding to shoot?" I ask, not satisfied with the direction our conversation went. She isn't wrong; I have been a playboy. I've never been in a relationship, but I'm not opposed to them, either. I just never found a woman I wanted to be in a relationship with.

"No, I need to finish setting up my office." Hazel grabs her purse off the chair she's sitting in and sets it in her lap.

"Where's your office?"

"Why?" She tilts her head to the side; her brown eyes penetrate me, trying to read my mind.

Because I'm not ready to stop trying to get to know you. "I'm curious. Is it a crime to try to get reacquainted with an old friend?"

"*Old friend?* Really? Jax, you don't remember who I am." This is true, but that doesn't mean I don't want to get to know her now.

"Why not? You're new in town, I'm fairly new in town. What's so wrong with being friends?"

"Ugh, fine. You're impossible." She throws her hands up. "I'm leaving now. Contrary to what Peter said, I am employed. I have my own business and that *is* employment." Hazel gulps the last of her coffee before standing and shouldering her purse.

"I believe you." I stand from the table. "So, where is this office of yours?"

"Why?" she asks over her shoulder as she walks to the door to exit *Sugar n' Sweet*.

"Do I need a reason?" I reach over her head and hold the door open for her before exiting out.

"Yes." She sighs, but stops outside the café and faces me. The sunlight is so bright on her golden skin, like she was made to be outside.

"I'm curious." I shrug.

"Not good enough." She smacks my shoulder. "You're going to follow me, aren't you?"

"Yep." I tuck my hands into my pockets and rock back on my heels. I wasn't going to follow, but it's a great idea.

"*Fine.* This way. It's not that far." She points over her shoulder. Hazel turns on her heels and heads toward her office. "I rent office space on the corner of Main and 1st Street."

"Main and 1st would be a good place to showcase your pictures." I nod, matching my stride with hers. "That's what you plan to do, right? Photography?"

"Booking photography gigs will help bring money in, but ultimately, I want to do graphic design work. Websites, logos, marketing material. There are a lot of local businesses here in Peak Valley that need their websites updated. I hope to convince a few places to rebrand themselves as well. Do you think you could talk to Clint about hiring me to update his website?"

Maybe I should believe in fate. "I can." I scratch my bearded chin, debating whether I should mention my need for a graphic artist so soon after the unsuccessful attempt to coax a date out of her. We walk in silence until we get close to her office before I ask, "Have you done a lot of graphic design work?"

"I was a graphic artist for a design firm in Kansas City before I moved back here," Hazel says while digging in her purse and stopping in front of a small office building with two large picture windows. "My specialty is logo design and branding, but I love creating websites. Here we are."

Looking through one of the big picture windows, I see a small conference room with several canvas photos of smiling couples, adorable kids, and a few landscapes. Through the other window is a large canvas of Amber and Luke on their wedding day with a stunning landscape behind them. It sits on an easel for those passing by to see. "What is the name of your business?"

"*Hazel Wood Designs.* I have a guy coming by in a few days to put my logo on the door."

Hazel unlocks the door but doesn't walk through it. "I designed it myself. Well… I guess I'll be seeing you."

"Actually…" I look over her head through her office to the backwall where her logo is hanging before I look down at her. "I want to hire you."

"I'm not taking your picture," Hazel groans, rolling her head back.

"I don't want my picture taken." I chuckle at her. "I need a graphic artist."

"Yeah right, Jax. I'm not falling for one of your jokes." Hazel narrows her eyes at me.

"One of my jokes?"

"You were always pulling jokes back in high school. I doubt that has changed with adulthood."

So, we went to high school together. How did I miss her?

"No joke. I'm opening a brewery here in Peak Valley. I need a graphic artist to design a logo for the brewery and my craft beers, build a website, and help design the menu. I should probably have some promotional material created as well."

"You're serious?"

"Yes, I'm serious. Who would joke about something like that?"

"You would!" She raises her arms in frustration and walks into her office.

"I promise I'm not joking; I need a graphic artist."

Hazel tucks her purse behind the desk that sits in the middle of the open office space. "A brewery?"

"*Colson Brewery*," I say, leaning a hip against the desk. "Luke has been remodeling Benny's old bar for me."

"You bought *Benny's Bar*? I miss his burgers." Hazel sits in the desk chair, nibbling her thumbnail and looking out one of the many picture windows.

"Want to come check it out?"

"The brewery? Now?"

"Yes, my brewery. It's a short walk."

Bells chime behind us as the door opens and Hazel stands. "Yo, jackwagon, what are you doing here?" Of course, Burns has to show up at the worst possible time. It's his superpower.

I point an accusing finger at him. "What are you doing here?"

"I'm here to see about a job. Did she finally agree to a date with you?" Burns asks, smiling innocently at Hazel, whose cheeks flush a bright red.

"We're friends, old man. And she isn't hiring," I growl with annoyance.

"Hey, you don't know if I'm hiring or not!" Hazel smacks my shoulder.

"Yeah, you don't know," Burns agrees, putting his hands on his hip. "I'm here about being a photographer."

"A photographer?" Hazel asks Burns, her eyes wide.

"Yeah, I want to be a photographer but only part-time, since I am retired after all." Burns is wearing his Polaroid camera around his neck and holds it up. "I even have my own camera."

"Burns…" I hiss his name, but Hazel lays a hand on my arm. It's a small touch, yet it soothes away my annoyance. She releases my arm sooner than I want and walks over to Burns.

"Oh wow, how old is this?" She points to his camera.

"I don't know. Found it in a car in my old junkyard." Burns runs a hand over it as if wiping dust off it.

"That's quite a find," Hazel says, then points at it. "Can I see it?"

"Sure." Burns pulls the strap over his head and flashes me a smug smile.

Bastard.

"It's heavier than I thought," Hazel comments, looking over every inch. "And it still works?"

"It does. She takes beautiful pictures." Burns tugs on his suspenders with a proud smile. He is going to brag about this moment for the rest of his life. "Janet found film on eBay. So, do I have a job?"

"Oh…" Hazel looks up from the camera at Burns. "I'm sorry… uh…"

"You can call me Burns." Burns sticks his hand out.

"Burns." Hazel nods and shakes his hand. "Thank you for stopping by, but I'm sorry, I'm not hiring." She hands back his camera. "I'm sorry, but hey, you can give me your number. If I need help with a photoshoot, I can give you a call."

"Thank you, dear." Burns takes the camera and looks over at me. "I got the job."

"You *maybe* got a job," I retort, crossing my arms over my chest. "And you interrupted me trying to hire her."

"You're hiring her? To do what?"

"I need a graphic artist, and she happens to be one."

"Graphic what? Is that what you call a photographer these days?"

"Are you two related?" Hazel points at the two of us.

"I claim him as mine when he isn't being a *jackwagon*," Burns answers, and despite my annoyance with him, it warms my chest. Burns has been more of a father to me than my own was. He tests my patience, can be nosy, and he's crazy, but I love him.

"We're family," I confirm.

"Well, thank you both for coming, but I should get to work." Hazel straightens her back.

"So, you'll take me on as a client?" I step toward her, a tiny bit of weight coming off my shoulders.

Hazel's smile falls and she blinks at me. "Can I think about it?"

Well, shit.

5

~ Hazel ~

I can't believe he stood me up. What kind of brother stands up his only sister? My brother, that's who. He could at least have sent a text.

"Here you go, hon." My waitress stirs me from my annoyed thoughts and sets a bag filled with Chinese take-out containers and the check onto my table.

"Thank you," I say and immediately hand her my card as my stomach growls from the scent of beef and broccoli penetrating my nose and making my mouth water.

"I'll be right back." The waitress winks at me and rushes off right as a short man about my age with thinning hair saunters up to my table.

"Hazel? Hazel Wood? Is that you?" he asks, taking a seat across from me before I can answer him. "I heard you were back in town."

"Um…" I bite my lip as I study his face. There is nothing remotely familiar about him.

"It's me, Johnny Davidson." He crosses his arms over the table and leans in. "You've changed… a lot."

I don't know this Johnny Davidson, and I can't tell if he is complimenting me or not. "Oh— "

"You changed for the better," he cuts me off, then throws in a wink. I'm not particularly fond of men who ask questions they don't expect an answer to, but Peak Valley is small and being rude to the wrong person can make or break your reputation. The last thing I need is another Peter Landers moment. Luckily, I haven't heard a peep about that disastrous encounter, and I hope it remains that way.

"Thank you," I say, wracking my brain for a clue to how Johnny knows me. He isn't a bad looking man, intrusive maybe, but his smile is genuine, if not flirty.

"Hazel Wood." He slaps the table, and I jump along with the condiments. It draws the attention of others. I never liked being the center of attention, and he's drawing other customer's attention. Being the center of attention is a source of anxiety for me and my go-to move is to flee, only I can't… not until the waitress returns. "I can't believe I ran into you. You know," he wiggles a finger at me, "I had the biggest crush on you when we were kids."

"Um… no, I didn't know that." *How could I? I don't remember who you are!* And I don't have the guts to ask either, but I'm sure we probably went to school together. Peak Valley may be small, but that doesn't mean I know everyone. Besides, I've been away for years. So much has changed.

"So, what have you been up to?"

"Oh, well… not much, you?"

He nods. "Same."

"Hey, Johnny," my waitress greets and drops my receipt and looks at me with a sympathetic smile. "Do you want me to get you a refill on your water?"

"No, thank you. I should get going. I'm meeting my brother." I snatch the receipt and stand.

"You can't leave yet. We were having such a great time catching up." Johnny stands and tugs on his jeans that look a bit too snug on him. I wouldn't exactly call this a good time.

"Oh darn. I guess we'll have to do this some other time." I shrug and give him an awkward wave.

"Wait." He stops me, entering into my personal space, and his cologne is strong and overbearing. "How about this Friday? We can have a drink at *The Two Step*."

"This Friday?" I breathe through my mouth and look around, noticing everyone in the room watching us, including the waitstaff. What is with the men of Peak Valley? First Jax and Peter cause a public scene, and now Johnny. Has this become the successful way to ask a girl out? Force them by not giving them a choice between a date or public humiliation.

"Yeah, this Friday. You can tell me what you've been up to, and I can buy my childhood crush a drink." He leans in and I can't tell if he's smelling my food or me, but his cologne is going to cause my eyes to burn. I need out and now.

"Where… where exactly is *The Two Step*?" I clutch my food and take a step back. The whole restaurant is silent as they wait for my decision.

"River Bend." Johnny steps forward and I step back, hitting my hip against the booth. "It'll be fun. Come on. Don't make me beg."

"Just drinks?" Drinks are harmless. And afterward, if I'm not interested—which will likely be the case—I can tell him privately, away from prying eyes. I did promise my mom I would try to put myself out there. It will be good practice.

"Just drinks." His smile widens, and he tucks his hands into his back pockets.

"Yeah. Okay. This Friday."

"Great, what's your number?" He pulls his phone out and taps in my number as I rattle it off. The patrons return to their foods and whisper to each other, and I can't tell if they are good whispers or not. "I'll pick you up at seven."

"Oh, I can meet you there."

"I'm old-school. I'll pick you up."

I hesitate but nod. "Okay. It was nice seeing you again."

"See you Friday."

My promise to my mother is turning into a headache.

*****

First, he stands me up, now he's keeping me waiting. The Chinese has to be cold by now.

"Excuse me." I step up to the Peak Valley Police Station desk where one of my brother's deputies has been eyeing me for the last twenty minutes. "Are you sure Warren knows I'm here?"

"He knows…" The deputy smoothers a smile, then glances over his shoulder before he leans in and whispers, "His dad is here, and Warren Sr. is pissed."

"Warren Sr. is here?" I swallow and glance over the deputy's shoulder to look into my brother's office. Through the glass, I see Warren Sr. pointing at my brother, yelling, his face red with anger.

"It might be a while before he can see you," the deputy says, turning back to face me.

"Maybe I should go." I glance at my watch. My lunch hour was over ten minutes ago; good thing I don't have any appointments scheduled for the afternoon.

The deputy turns to watch Warren and his father once more, leaning against the station desk. "Maybe not, looks like he's losing steam."

"I'm not sure I want to stick around after Warren Sr. rips my brother a new one." I frown.

The deputy laughs. "You're funny."

I am? "Thanks. I think." I've never been called funny. I never once thought of myself as funny. Shy yes, quiet yes, but funny…?

"Your food must be cold. How about you let me buy you dinner later?" The deputy leans in, and my mouth falls open before I promptly shut it. I scan his chest, L. Waugh. "I'm Leo." He runs a hand beneath his name.

"Hi, Leo." I smile, hoping he doesn't notice my flushed cheeks. Leo is definitely better looking than Johnny Davidson. Taller, a little thick, with a clean shave and cropped hair. "I'm Hazel."

"I know. And you're my boss' little sister." He chuckles and leans in closer, waving me forward as if he has a secret to share.

"That doesn't worry you?"

"Not a bit." He winks and sits his chin on his fist, flashing me a flirty smile. Do I have a sign over my head that says eligible? Two dates in one day can't be a coincidence. "So, what do you say? I get off at six. We can get a bite around seven."

"Tonight?"

"Unless another day works better for you. Maybe Friday?"

Crap, I can't tomorrow. I have another date… Wait, is getting drinks a date? "No, tonight works."

"Great." He straightens, pride radiating from him and warming my chest. Maybe if things go well tonight, I can cancel on Johnny tomorrow.

"So… um, do you want my number?" I throw out, feeling confident. After all, I have two… er, one and half dates.

"Yes, ma'am." He pulls his phone from his chest pocket. After he saves it and sends me a text, the station door flies open and a red-faced Warren Sr. storms out, not even sparing a glance my way.

"Crap, Hazel, I forgot we were meeting for lunch." Warren rubs his forehead.

"It's okay." I shrug and walk to where I was sitting earlier to pick up the cold Chinese food. "Want to heat it up?"

"Sure." He sighs, and I hesitate.

"Are you sure?"

"Yeah, c'mon." Warren opens the door and waves me through.

"See you later tonight," Leo calls out. Warren gives me a quizzical look as we navigate through his deputies' desks to the small breakroom at the back.

"What was that all about?" Warren nods toward Leo and my cheeks flush again. I wish I didn't blush so easily—a symptom of being shy, and an embarrassing one at that.

"We're having dinner later," I say, pulling his lo mein out and tossing it into the microwave with a smug smile.

"I see." Warren sucks his lips in with a little cough that sounds a lot like a laugh.

"What is so funny about me having a date?"

"Not laughing at you having a date, but *who* you have a date with." Warren rubs the back of his neck, failing to hold back a smirk.

"What's wrong with Leo?"

"Nothing, he's a good deputy."

"What's he like as a man?" I demand, putting my hands on my hips and narrowing my eyes at him.

Warren looks up at the ceiling and ponders for a moment.

"*What?*"

"He's a talker and a momma's boy, but harmless. I'm sure you'll have a great time," Warren finally shares as the microwave beeps.

"I'm also having drinks with Johnny Davidson tomorrow," I add, opening the microwave and stirring up the food before turning it back on.

"Johnny Davidson… I don't know him." Warren frowns.

"He grew up in Peak Valley…" I leave out that I don't really know him, either. It's a minor detail—one that Warren will only overreact to.

"Hmm." Warren crosses his arms and leans his back against the counter. "Two dates in two days. Are you turning into a serial dater?"

"Serial dater? What the heck is that?" I scrunch my nose at him.

"Apparently you." Warren elbows me with a grin.

"I'm putting myself out there, what's wrong with that?" I elbow back.

"Has anyone else asked you out?"

"No…" I frown, not sure if Jax counts. He didn't exactly ask me out. He flirted before we settled on being friends, and now he wants to hire me. I just don't know if I can trust myself to be professional and not crush on him. It would be too easy to fall for Jax.

"A certain Colson didn't try?"

"Jax Colson?" I play dumb and side-eye my brother, who narrows his eyes at me. I don't know why I bother trying to hide anything from him—he can read me like a book.

"Yeah, Jax Colson. He was asking about you at the wedding."

"He did?" I ask, biting my cheek so I don't let the smile break out across my face. This is why I can't work for him.

"He tried, didn't he?" Warren swears under his breath, and I wonder what that's all about. Isn't he friends with the Colsons now?

"No, not exactly, but he did ask if I would take him on as a client," I offer on a sigh and run my hands through my hair. The work he wants me to do is exactly the kind of work I want *Hazel Wood Designs* to be known for. *Colson Brewery* could really set me on a path for success, but not if I blow it because I don't know how to be professional around my childhood crush. "He wants me to do some graphic design work for him. It's an amazing opportunity, but I'm not sure if I will take it."

"I see." Warren's mouth pinches together.

"What do you think?" We may not have been close growing up and only just starting to build a relationship, but I have always wanted my brother's opinion. Valued it, even when it isn't the opinion I want to hear.

"I think you need to be careful with him. He isn't exactly your type."

"Trust me, I know he isn't my type." I laugh, thinking of all the women Jax used to date when we were in high school. "But working for him doesn't mean dating him."

"I know. If you aren't sure, then don't accept his offer. Other offers will come."

"I hope so." I bite my thumb. Jax's has been the only promising graphic design work I've received. There are several businesses in Peak Valley that are interested in my services, but no one has booked anything. I'm trying not to worry; I did just start the business and they say the first year is always the hardest.

"Hang in there. It'll happen." Warren squeezes my shoulder. "And be careful with all these guys you're dating. I know Mom wants you to get married before she's too..." he doesn't finish the sentence. Both of us haven't been able to say the words out loud. Alzheimer's is a terrible disease.

"She told you?" I straighten and cover my mouth when I realized I asked too loudly, drawing attention to us.

"She wanted me to hook you up with one of my deputies, but you beat me to it," Warren teases.

"I can't believe she told you," I groan and lean back against the counter, looking up at the yellowing ceiling tiles.

"She'll be happy to know you're getting yourself out there, but tone it down some. You'll get a reputation."

"It just *happened*," I defend. "I wasn't exactly putting myself out there. The last time I put myself out there was with Peter, and that was a disaster."

"I heard about that." Warren nods, watching his deputies as they meander around.

"You *did*?" I face him in horror.

"He's an asshole, don't freak." The microwave beeps and Warren turns to pull the food out.

"How did you hear about it?" I hiss, opening my container of beef and broccoli and popping it into the microwave.

"Mom." Warren laughs, twirling his lo mein with his fork before shuffling it into his mouth.

"How did *she* hear about it?"

"I have no idea." Warren shrugs.

"Small-town living is bad for my health," I grumble.

"It was your choice to move back," Warren says, then winces.

"Thanks for making me feel welcome, big brother," I retort, and stir my food before heating it up some more.

"I didn't mean it like that…" he tries to apologize, and I know he didn't mean it. Warren was never good with his words, but even unintentionally, they hurt. We stand in awkward silence, waiting for my food to heat up.

"How did you mean it? You haven't exactly been supportive of my decision."

"I support you, Hazel." Warren sighs with a bite of annoyance in his tone. "I just didn't want you to make an impulsive decision that you'll regret. You were happy in Kansas City, had a good job. I want you to be happy."

His words cause tears to sting the back of my eyes. Not once did I think he was concerned about my happiness. I assumed he didn't want me around like he didn't want me around when we were younger. Did I have it all wrong all these years?

"C'mon, let's eat in my office." He nods toward his office, unaware that he completely blew my mind. "Unless you want another one of my deputies to ask you out."

"Funny," I say with a half-smile, following him to his office. "So, why was your dad here? He looked... upset?"

"Upset?" Warren chortles. "He was pissed."

"What was he pissed about?"

Warren grits his teeth, dropping his food onto his desk and taking a seat while I sit in one of his guest chairs. "He wanted me to arrest Forest James."

"That's a name I haven't heard in a while... I thought he cleaned up his act." I raise a concerned brow. Warren doesn't talk about the James family. It's been a forbidden subject since Lily James, the love of his life, disappeared.

"As far as I know, he's never been in trouble. He used to hang with the wrong crowd back when we were kids, but he mostly stayed out of trouble. Pops has dirt on Forrest, but the statute of limitations makes it impossible for me to do anything about it."

"That's odd." I munch on the end of a broccoli stem. "Why now?"

"Lily James returned to Peak Valley. Her mother just passed away."

"I thought she was missing." I arch a surprised brow at him. I was too young to understand what was happening, but not so young that I didn't see how perfect Lily and Warren were together. I saw her as a sister and missed her terribly.

Warren looks out the window with his jaw clenched. "She was never missing."

"What does her return have to do with your dad wanting to put Forest away?"

"I haven't figured that out yet." Warren wipes his mouth with a napkin and throws it onto the desk.

"Have you seen her?"

"I saw her at her mother's funeral." He nods, leaning back in his chair and steepling his fingers. I may not know my brother as well as I would like, but I know when he isn't telling me everything.

"Just the funeral?"

"I may have pulled her over…" Warren sighs in frustration.

"That was a stupid move," I scoff. Warren has a tendency to pull over people he wants to annoy.

"You almost finished?" He presses his lips together. Clearly, I hit a cord.

"No." I give him a pointed stare while taking a small bite of rice.

He narrows his eyes. "Well, I've got work to do."

"More like a conversation to avoid," I push back.

"Fine, I'm avoiding conversation." He runs a hand down his face. "I just spent the last hour getting my ass chewed by Pops over the James family, and I'm tired of talking about them. Can we leave it at that?"

"Fair enough, big brother." I give him a sympathetic smile and grab the container lid for my food. "I'm here to listen or talk if you need it."

"Thanks." He chin-lifts as I stand to leave.

"Don't be too hard on Lily James. You don't know her story," I remind him. We were all surprised by her disappearance, but after the shock wore off, we all saw a change in Warren. Lily James took his heart with her. Now that she's back, I hope he will give her the benefit of the doubt. The old Warren would have, but heartbroken Warren started to turn more into Warren Sr., and Warren Sr. never gave anyone the benefit of the doubt.

Picture Forever

6

~ Jax ~

Hazel is *talented*. I looked through her portfolio over the last couple of days, but I wanted to see more than just pieces she created for herself. I wanted to see the work she's done for others, which was harder to come by. I tried to find the firm she worked for to see if I could get anything from them, but with several graphic design firms in Kansas City, it was impossible to know for sure if I was looking at something Hazel had created. That is, until I made a quick call to my brother's computer expert Cricket. I offered a case of my Spicy Bumpkin seasonal beer for Hazel's portfolio and Cricket's silence. The last thing I need is for Eric to know what I'm up to. It'll undoubtably get back to McKnight. Cricket, being the genius she is, had compiled a list of clients Hazel created logos, branding campaigns, and websites for in less than a day.

Her talent is by far the best I've seen. Not that the other graphic artist I worked with weren't talented. They were, but Hazel's art is on another level. I was blown away by her ability to capture a business owner's personality and encases it in their brand. It's exactly what I've been looking for.

The tricky part is convincing her to take me on as a client. She may have asked for time to think about it, but she was honest about trying to avoid me as well. It may have been her polite way of getting rid of me, only so she can ghost me later. Luckily, I have a plan. One that consists of a variety pack of my hand-crafted beers, a tasty pizza fresh from the stonefire oven, and my relentless desire to get to know the intriguing, brown-eyed woman who has managed to elude me.

"Welcome to *Hazel Wood Designs…*" Hazel frowns from behind the lobby desk. "Jax, hi."

"I come baring gifts." I raise my arm, holding the still-hot pizza. "I wanted to give you a taste of what you'll be working with."

"I haven't decided to work with you yet." She bites her lip, her eyes zeroing in on the pizza. It does smells delicious.

"Consider this a form of bribery, although my food and beer sell themselves." I wink as I place the beer and pizza on the lobby desk.

"It does smell good…" She lifts her chin to get a better look at the pizza as I open the box lid, letting the savory smell of tomato sauce and cheese invade her space.

"Trust me, it tastes better than it smells." I pull out a bottle of Melon Choly Ale and crack it open.

She takes the beer and reads the crude label. "Melon Choly Ale?"

"It's a red ale with watermelon and ginger," I say and watch as she smells it but doesn't try it. "Try it."

Hazel bites her lip again before smelling it one more time, then she brings the bottle to her mouth and takes a tiny sip.

"Take another sip. Trust me, it's good," I push. "It really is a good beer, and I'm not tooting my own horn. I made it for women who aren't normally beer drinkers."

Hazel looks over the bottle for several seconds. She looks ready to decline it, but then she surprises me as she brings it back to her lips and takes a drink. The corner of her lip twitches, but she quickly suppresses it before taking another drink and my heart skips a beat. I need to her like my beer. It's crucial for her to like it and the food. If she likes it, I have no doubt she can bring my vision into my brand.

"This is good," she says, looking inside the bottle.

"You sound surprised." I chuckle and grab a napkin to place a slice of pizza on it.

"I am actually. I never knew watermelon would taste good in beer," she admits and puts the beer down and takes the pizza.

"Neither did I until I tried it." I smile and watch her pick at the cheese on the pizza before smelling it.

"You made this?"

"I did." I nod, and then push the pizza closer to her mouth—a beautiful mouth at that.

Hazel glares at me, but takes a bite. She chews twice before her eyes widen and she smiles while still chewing. "This is good," she hums and takes another bite.

"My sister-in-law Dawn helped me perfect it," I tell her. "You met her."

"I remember. She's married to your monster truck-sized brother."

"That's her." I laugh at her description of Clint.

"Mmm," she groans as she takes another bite, and I never thought watching someone eat pizza could look sexy. Today she isn't wearing a sundress I'm used to seeing her in; instead, she opted for a pair of skinny jeans and an oversized, lightweight sweater. Her hair is pulled into a ponytail, and she is fresh-faced for late in the day. I don't know how I missed her in high school. I would have talked to her. I would have tried to get to know her.

"Do you want to try the Stout It Out beer?" I ask and pull out another bottle.

"I want another slice," she says, stuffing the last bite of pizza into her mouth.

"I'm glad you like it." I move to get her another slice.

"Wait. What time is it?" She stops me and looks at her watch. "No, I can't. I have to go."

"Trying to avoid me again?"

"No, I have a date. I need to get home and change." She crumbles the napkin and walks around the lobby desk and throws it away.

"A date?" Who the hell is she dating now? And how did he weasel his way in? She's doing her best to avoid me, but every other guy in Peak Valley doesn't appear to be off limits.

"Yes," she says and shuts the lid of her laptop and unplugs it before looking up at me. "Thank you for letting me sample your pizza and beer. It was really good."

"Why do I feel a *but* coming?"

"No buts, I just want to think more about taking you on as a client. Can we talk about this another time?"

"When?"

"Umm…" She looks down at her laptop, then back at her watch. "I'll get back with you on that, but I have to go or I'm going to be late."

I want to protest, stall her, do anything to stop her from leaving. I'm not opposed to using trickery, but I need her. I need her to bring my vision to life, so I nod, pack up, and leave. Chasing Hazel is becoming a challenge unlike any I've ever tackled. I'm not used to not getting what I want and it's driving me crazy.

*****

"Oh, good Jax, I'm glad you are here," Amber calls from the kitchen, looking frazzled when I walk through the front door of her remodeled dream home. "Do you mind running to *Alejandro's* and pick up dinner? I just called in a carry-out order."

"Getting lazy now that you're married?" I ask and come into the kitchen and kiss her cheek.

"Get your grubby hands off my wife," Luke says as he comes into the kitchen with my nephew Matt.

"Make me." I pick up Amber and carry her around the island as she screeches at me.

"Put me down!" She squirms out of my arms and playfully shoves me. "Man child!"

"You love this man child." I laugh and duck a smack from Luke, who pulls Amber into his arms. "Where is everyone else?"

"They should be here soon," Amber says, wrapped in Luke's arms. "Dawn is bringing *tres leches* for dessert."

"Do you want me to get it now?"

"Yes, please."

"Can I go with you, Uncle Jax?" Matt asks, coming to stand in front of me.

"If your mom says it's okay." I smile down at Matt. He grows taller every time I see him. Soon he will be less of a child and more of a teen. I don't envy Luke and Amber if he is anything like my brothers and I were when we were teenagers.

"Fine with me. Jax is going to need your help carrying all the food I ordered."

"Awesome!"

"Let's jet." I hitch my thumb toward the front door and wave at Amber and Luke as we leave.

Matt and I jam out to heavy metal on the short drive to *Alejandro's*. The kid can head bang, and I like having these moments with them. It helps solidify the favorite uncle title.

Alejandro's is surprisingly packed for a Thursday night, and if Amber ordered a feast worthy enough to feed my brothers, then we may be here for a while.

"Are you excited for Dawn's *tres leches*?" Matt asks as we walk into *Alejandro's*.

"I am, are you?"

"Yes," Matt says, opening the door to *Alejandro's*.

"Hi, table for two?" the hostess greets us as we walk up to the hostess stand.

"We're here for a pick-up order under the name Amber Colson." I flash a friendly smile.

"Okay, I see your order. It will be just a few minutes. Do you mind taking a seat and I'll bring your order out to you when it's ready?"

"Thanks." I smile and head for the bench of seats close to the door.

"Psst, Jax." I hear someone call my name and look around at tables. No one is looking at me. I know a few of the people here, but none that would be trying to get my attention.

"Uncle Jax, I think that photographer lady is calling you." Matt taps me and points toward the bathrooms to the right.

"Jax, come here." Hazel waves me over with wide-eyed desperation. She's hiding behind a half-open restroom door and waves urgently at me. "Hurry!"

"Wait here, Matt," I tell my nephew and walk over to Hazel. "Fancy meeting you here."

"I need your help." She grabs my shirt and pulls me into the restroom, slamming the door shut.

"What kind of help?" I raise a brow at her with a flirty smile.

She ignores my flirting. "I need you to get me out of this date."

"Excuse me?"

"I'm on a date with one of my brother's deputies, and he brought his *mom*!" She raises her arms in disbelief. "His *mom*!"

"His mom?"

"Yes, that's what I said." She slaps her hands on her hips. "She won't stop talking about him."

"So leave." I shrug nonchalantly.

"I *tried*!" she huffs, nibbling on her thumb. "I tried to say my stomach hurt, and his mom gave me some Pepto."

"Is that why it smells in here?" I scrunch my nose.

"No!" She smacks my chest. "I need you to help me get out of this. I'm afraid if I stay any longer, Leo's mom will announce our engagement. She's already told me she thinks we'll have beautiful babies. I need you to think of something that will get me out of this."

"Let me get this straight…" I tap a finger to my lips. "You want *me* to come up with a brilliant idea that will get *you* out of a date you are currently on. Do I have it right?"

"Yes," she huffs, narrowing her eyes at me.

"What's in it for me?"

"In it for you?"

"Yeah." I nod my head.

"What do you want?"

"Agree to do my branding. All of it."

Hazel sucks in a breath and holds it before letting it out. "Okay, fine. I'll do your branding, but only if you get me out of this."

"You've got yourself a deal." I smirk and hold out my hand.

Hazel wraps her hand in mine and grumbles, "Thank you."

"Go sit down and I'll come find you." I open the bathroom door and push her out of it.

Hazel gives me a pleading look before walking away and out of sight. I wait a moment before going back to Matt. "I'm going to need your help, bud. You up for some fun?"

"Always," Matt says without hesitation.

"You saw Hazel walk by?" Matt nods and looks over at the table where she's sitting. "We need to come up with an excuse to get her out of her date."

"Why does she want to get out of her date?"

"He brought his mom." I aim for the simplest explanation.

"Why?"

"I don't know, but we need to come up with something. Got any ideas?"

"Um, we could say... her dog got out."

"I don't think she has a dog."

"Does her date know that?"

"No clue, but let's roll with it. You up for it?" I hold my hand up.

"Yes." Matt high fives me.

"Alright, look alive and follow me." I stand and lead Matt toward the table where Hazel is sitting in front of an older women in her mid-fifties. She's chatting away, giving her son doe-eyes.

"Hazel, I'm glad I found you!" I say, laying a hand on her shoulder and smiling down at her. "Matt found your dog wandering the streets, lost."

"Oh dear, your poor dog," the older woman says clutching her chest. "My Leo got me a dog after my dear husband passed away. The cutest schnauzer I ever did see. Isn't that right, Leo."

"He's a good dog. I know my dogs." Leo nods, not bothering to look up from his food.

I open my mouth to speak, but Leo's mom beats me to it. "What kind of dog do you have, Hazel?"

"Oh, um…" Hazel's wide brown eyes look at me for help.

"A German Shephard," Matt answers with a smile.

"Did you hear that, Leo? A German Shephard." Leo's mom elbows her son, then points at Hazel with a knowing smile. "I knew I had a good feeling about you, Hazel."

"About your dog…" I squeeze her shoulder. "You should come get him."

"What is your dog's name?" Leo's mom asks, unperturbed by my presence. I can't tell if she knows what she's doing or if she is just a chatty woman.

"My dog's name… is um… dog?" Hazel winces and I bite back a laugh.

"Dog? Why would you name it dog?"

"Oh… because, um… I thought a simple name would make training him easier," Hazel stutters, and it doesn't take a genius to see the lie written across her face. The scene is comical, and I bite my cheek to hold back the smile threatening to break free.

"I suppose that makes senses." Leo's mom frowns but perks up and puts her fork down. "I named my schnauzer Winston. I wanted him to have a strong name, like my son."

"Winston is a strong name," Leo chimes in, his mouth full of food. Hazel doesn't deserve his disinterest and it's grating on my nerves.

"I hate to interrupt, but I think Hazel should really come with us to get her dog." I smile innocently at Leo's mom.

"He's really scared and whining," Matt adds.

"German Shephards don't get scared, boy." Leo's mom shakes her head. "They are fearless creatures, they are. Ain't that right, Leo?"

"They are." Leo nods and looks at Matt. "You should put him back where you found him."

Matt frowns and jerks his head back. "Wouldn't that make him lost again?"

"German Shephards are smart dogs. He'll find his way home," Leo's mom says.

"I really think you should come get your dog," I insist and clench my jaw to stop from laughing at the ridiculousness Leo and his mom are suggesting.

"I think you're right." Hazel nods and pushes back from the table. "Thank you so much for dinner. I'm sorry, but I must cut it short."

"You haven't touched your meal, Hazel. Did the Pepto not help your stomach?"

"No, it hasn't helped." Hazel stands, clutching her stomach.

"You poor thing. Sensitive stomachs are a sign of sickness. You aren't sick, are you?"

"I don't think so." Hazel pulls the strap of her purse over her shoulder, and I'm about to grab her and run just to get away from the endless chatter.

"My Leo never gets sick. Has been as healthy as a horse since the day he was born. Right, Leo?"

"Yeah," Leo says while wiping his mouth with his napkin. "I can finish her meal."

"Thank—"

"Are you two going Dutch? I heard that is what you young people do these days," Leo's mom asks while reaching over to grab Hazel's plate and hands it to Leo.

"Going Dutch?" I raise an eyebrow at Leo, who is already digging into Hazel's food.

"Split the bill, but don't worry about paying for me. My Leo always pays for me. He's a gentleman."

"Oh, um… sure, I can pay for my meal." Hazel unzips her purse, but I stop her and pull my wallet out and take a twenty and drop it onto the table.

"That should cover Hazel. It was a pleasure talking with you both. Have a nice dinner." I nod at them both, then wrap a hand around Hazel's elbow and gently pull her away from the table before Leo's mom can say anything more.

"You didn't have to pay for me," Hazel hisses, picking up her pace.

"What kind of asshole asks a woman out on a date and then makes her pay for it?" I mutter before we get to the hostess stand.

"Thank you," Hazel says with relief in her voice as she glances over her shoulder at Leo and his mom. "I appreciate it, Jax."

"Pick up for Amber?" The hostess holds up one of the bags. "There are three other bags."

"Thank you," I tell the hostess, taking one of the bags she's holding up and hand it over to Matt. Hazel takes a bag from me I pass to her, and I gather the rest of the bags.

Hazel is at the door holding it open and I smile when she waves at me to hustle. "Hurry up!"

"Got somewhere to be?" I smirk at her.

"Yes." She rolls her eyes. "I have a fictional dog to rescue."

"Who names their fictional dog, dog?" Matt asks with a teasing smile.

"Yeah, Hazel?" I laugh. "I thought you were supposed to be creative."

"I don't deal well under pressure. It was the first thing I could think of," Hazel groans but smiles.

"Can you pull my keys out of my pocket?" I turn to face Hazel when we get to my truck.

She rolls her eyes at me, holding her hand out. "Hand me your bag."

"Nothing's in there that will bite." I chuckle and hand her the bag.

"I don't believe you." She takes the bag and walks around me. "You can sit in the front," she says to Matt.

"Are you sure?" He rubs the back of his neck with a shy smile.

"Absolutely." She nods, and I smile as I unlock the truck and we pile in. I have Hazel exactly where I want her. No more avoiding me now.

Picture Forever

7

~ Hazel ~

I can't believe I'm sitting in Jax's truck on my way home from the worst date I have ever been on. Not only was it the worst date, but I had to be rescued by *Jax*. He has a habit of showing up to bear witness to my humiliation. I'm going to need a whole bottle of wine and a bubble bath to wash away my embarrassment.

My street zips by and I sit up and tap Jax's shoulder. "You missed my turn."

Jax glances at me through the rearview mirror. "I know."

Okay...? "Are you going to turn around?"

He shakes his head and looks straight ahead. "Nope."

I lean forward to see where he's driving us. "Where are you taking me?" We are heading into an older neighborhood not far from where I grew up.

"To Amber and Luke's," Jax says, and I sit up straighter.

"Why?"

"You need to eat."

I cross my arms and glare at the back of his head. "First you twist my arm, and now you're holding me hostage so you can feed me?"

"Don't be so dramatic." Jax laughs, grinning at me from the rearview mirror. "You didn't touch your meal, and we have plenty of food. And I didn't twist your arm."

"Then what would you call it?"

"*Bartering.*"

"Always full of jokes," I mutter and lean against the window.

Matt turns in his seat to smile at me. "Dawn is bringing *tres leches* for dessert."

"Dawn is coming?" I glance at Jax for confirmation.

"Yeah, everyone is coming." Matt nods. "Mom and Luke just got back from their honeymoon."

"There better be wine," I grumble, watching the houses pass by. I like Amber and Luke. I enjoyed being the photographer at their wedding, even enjoyed getting to know them and their family. But being in Jax's presence shakes my confidence, and I don't trust myself not to make a mistake like kiss him, only for things to get awkward when he gets his fill of me and moves on.

"There will be wine. Have you met my brothers' wives?" Jax lets out a sarcastic laugh.

Jax pulls up to a cute, white two-story home with an inviting red door that I immediately adore. It's the kind of home I could see myself living in, starting a family in, and growing old in, but I need a partner to have all those things and I'm failing miserably in the dating department.

Several cars line the street around the home as Jax pulls into the driveway and parks. Matt jumps out and heads for the house before I have an opportunity to climb out of the truck. I lean across the seat, reaching for the food when I feel Jax at my back. He's close enough I can feel the warmth of his body. He reaches in and takes the bags off the seat but doesn't step away. A flush spreads from the top of my head to the tips of my toes, and my stomach churns with a million butterflies.

"You smell good," he whispers close to my ear, the rumble of his voice vibrating through me, and I fight the urge to lean into him.

"Th-thank you," I murmur, unable to move, yet wishing he would move closer.

Jax clears his throat and I turn my head slightly. He's looking down at my neck with an intensity that spikes my heartrate and fills me with a sense of power. A man has never stared at me so intently before, as if I'm the only cure to his desire. Curiosity pushes aside my self-preservation and shyness, and I lift my chin, giving Jax access to my mouth.

"Yo, jackwagon, what's taking so long? We're starving in here," Burns yells from the front porch. My curiosity—and bravery—disappears, and I turn away from Jax, my body temperature elevating to volcanic levels.

"Coming," Jax yells back but doesn't step away, and the hair on the back of my neck tingles. I feel his warm breath against my ear. "Ready?" A featherlight touch against the shell of my ear sends all the volcanic heat straight to my core, and I sway on my feet. I've lost my voice and stand there silent, rooted where I am. I don't know if he steps away sensing my unease or not, but I have never been more thankful for the cool air.

I step away from the truck and Jax slams my door shut. I don't look at him, too scared I'll lose my wits and self-control—something I can't afford to do when I'm around Jax. Forget wine and a bubble bath, I'm going to need a cold shower when I get home.

*****

"I'm so glad Jax ran into you," Amber says taking the seat next to me. "Matt said your date brought his mom...?"

"He did." I nod, glancing to my right where Sarah is sitting, resting her hands on her very pregnant belly. "Do you want me to get you something to eat?"

"No, Eric is getting it for me." She smiles and looks over her shoulder where the men are scooping heaps of food onto their plates. I thought Jax picked up a feast, but now I'm worried there won't be enough food. "Who brings their mother to a date?"

"Leo Waugh, I guess," I mutter, briefly closing my eyes and shaking my head. Matt let everyone know he and Jax rescued me before I entered the house, so everyone was waiting to greet me and pepper me with a million questions until Jax suggested we get our food before it got cold.

"Deputy Waugh?" Eric asks, placing a plate in front of Sarah and handing her utensils.

"That's the one." I nod with unease.

"Does your brother know?" Eric asks, tilting his head to the side looking surprised.

"Yes…"

"Interesting." He raises his brows.

"Why is that interesting?" Amber asks as she uncorks a wine bottle and pours some into my wine glass. If I knew her better, I would hug her.

"Nope, not answering that." Eric laughs and walks away.

"What did your brother say about you going out with Leo?" Amber asks, moving to fill her wine glass to the brim. Since arriving, Amber, Sarah, and Dawn have tried to make me feel welcome, but I still feel awkward crashing their family dinner.

"He laughed." I grimace. "Now I know why."

"That's horrible. Do you want me to have Eric punch him?" Sarah asks with a sympathetic smile. "He'll do it. I can ask him for anything while I'm at the end of my pregnancy. It's the best thing about being pregnant."

"No. No, I don't want Eric to get in trouble. Even if Warren deserves it." I look up at her shocked.

"Nah, Eric wouldn't get in trouble, but I will give Warren the cold shoulder if you want. We're Team Hazel."

"Team Hazel?"

"She means we've got your back." Dawn laughs.

"Oh… um… thank you." I bite my lip, touched by their kindness.

"You should go on a date with Jax. He wouldn't bring his mom," Emily, Amber's daughter, suggests. "Can he bring me? I want to go on a date."

"You're never going on a date," Luke calls from the other end of the long table where the men are taking their seats.

"Why not?" Emily frowns.

"Because I said so."

"Mom, can I go on a date with Jax and Hazel?"

"Sure, dear, if they say it's okay."

"Oh no." I swallow a large bite of food and cough as it nearly chokes me. "Jax and I aren't going on a date."

"Why not?" Emily asks, her eyes growing wide with a puppy dog pout.

"Because… we aren't," I stumble with the answer and not dare to glance at Jax, though I feel his eyes on me.

"Because why?" Emily asks with a hint of a whine in her voice. I look to Amber for help.

Amber pats her little arm. "Emily, you can't force people on dates."

"Why not? I forced you and Luke on a date and now you're married," Emily points out.

Good Lord, is she not an adorable spitfire. I can't really argue with her logic, even if I don't know what she's talking about.

"Emily, remember when we talked about you being bossy?" Amber asks, lowering her voice so it's harder for others to hear.

"Yes." She nods, looking at her mom with a frown. "It isn't polite to tell people what to do…"

"You have to let Hazel and Jax decide to go on a date." Amber runs a hand over Emily's glossy brown hair. "Okay?"

"Okay, Mom." Emily slumps her shoulders. "Sorry, Hazel," Emily sniffs, looking down at her food. "You don't *have* to go on a date with Jax."

I have no idea what to say to her, but I'm ready to agree to go on a date if it will take that sad, puppy dog look off her face. "It's okay, Emily."

"Welcome to the Colson clan," Sarah whispers at my side, and I give her a quizzical look. "Jax likes you. He can't take his eyes off you." She glances at Jax, who is talking to Clint, seemingly unperturbed by what just happened.

"Oh, no. It's not like that at all." I adamantly shake my head. "Amber should give Jax the bossy speech. He totally tricked me into coming here."

"That sounds like Jax." Dawn smiles over her water glass. "How'd he trick you?"

"The only way he would help me escape Leo and his mom was if I agreed to do his branding for his brewery."

"Oh, I bet you will create something amazing." Amber pats my hand. "You are very talented."

"Thank you."

"If Jax gives you trouble, call us." Sarah pats my shoulder. "Remember, we're Team Hazel."

"You guys are too kind." I let out a breath and relax my shoulders. It's nice being around women who are so caring. I've never had many friends, and the ones I did have were surface-level friends or acquaintances. I've longed for real friendships, the kind that last forever, but never knew how to forge a relationship. My shyness was perceived wrong. Where others thought I was standoffish, these ladies don't seem to notice it. It isn't an obstacle that they will let stop them from trying to be my friend, and I have never felt more grateful.

"Shut it, you jackwagon," Burns growls from the end of the table, breaking me from my thoughts.

"What'd I say?" Jax asks, holding his hands up. I know that look—the fake innocence look. His eyes always give him away. They hold a mischievous glint you can't help but smile at.

"Stop making me look bad in front of my future boss. I'm trying to be *professional.*" Burn throws his napkin at Jax.

"Future boss?" Sarah swivels her head between Burns and me. "You're hiring Burns?"

"When she has some work where she needs some help, she said I can be her assistant." Burns puffs his chest out with a proud smile. I did say that, but I didn't realize how important it was to him. "But this *jackwagon* is trying to make me look bad."

"I'm not trying to make you look bad." Jax rolls his eyes and tosses the napkin back at Burns. "I just asked why you're so quiet. It isn't like you."

"Stop riling Burns up." Luke smacks the back of Jax's head, and I snort over my wine glass. Jax narrows his eyes at me for a moment before I cough and look away, trying to hide my smile.

"If you haven't noticed, this place can turn into a zoo." Amber smiles with a wink as the men start to bicker. "I hope we don't scare you away."

"I'm usually the one scaring people away."
I put my wine glass down after gulping the last of
it.

"You? No." Dawn laughs, ignoring the
men at the end of the table.

"I do." I let out a deep breath, liquid
courage letting my words fly off my tongue. "I'm
socially awkward, shy, and apparently prone to
humiliation."

"You aren't socially awkward," Dawn
protests with a knowing smile. "Maybe a little shy,
but that's nothing we can't cure."

"She's right," Sarah chimes in. "Dawn was
shy once. She barely said a word, but look at her
now. You can't get her to shut up." Sarah laughs
then winces, shifting in her seat.

"You okay?" Eric stops his conversation
with his brothers, giving Sarah his full attention.

"Fine." Sarah waves him off. "She just
kicked me."

Eric studies Sarah for several seconds
before reluctantly turning back to his brothers.
"The Colson men like to hover a lot, too," she
adds. "Get used to it."

They talk about the Colson men as if I'm
already in a relationship with Jax. I'm excited about
starting a friendship with these women, really

excited, but will they still want to be friends when they realize Jax and I will never happen—no matter how infatuated I am with him. He's a client now, and my number one rule is to *never* date a client.

*****

Drinks with Johnny Davidson will not be another humiliating date… almost date. Is getting drinks considered a date? My mind has been racing since he picked me up. I'm nervous and overthinking. We haven't spoken a word to each other since I climbed into his car. Music blasted through the speakers, and he sang to it with more enthusiasm than a karaoke singer—for the entire thirty-minute drive to *The Two Step*. I enjoy singing along to a catchy song, but shouldn't we be talking to each other? I thought having drinks meant getting to know each other, but so far all I've learned about Johnny is that he sings off-key.

When we walked into *The Two Step,* we were blasted with more music, and I haven't been able to hear a single word he's said to me. The closest I've got to a conversation with him is a nod. The bar was packed, but Johnny managed to order two beers while we stood around for a while until a table in a dark corner at the back of the bar became available. The table still had empty glasses and beer bottles when we sat down, but I'm not complaining. I should have never worn heels.

I opted for a little black dress and realized the moment I stepped through the door that I was overdressed for *The Two Step*. I should have changed when Johnny pulled up wearing a pair of worn jeans and a faded anime shirt, but I was too shy to speak up.

Johnny leans in and yells into my ear, "Do you want another drink?"

I look down at my beer that's not even half empty, but the crowd around the bar will take a while for Johnny to wade through so I yell back to get me another, but then I jerk away when he squeezes my butt.

"Be right back." He winks and leaves me standing, stunned and alone in a dark corner at a table I don't dare set my purse on.

I knew before arriving to at *The Two Step* there wouldn't be a second date with Johnny, but I wanted to have fun, break my humiliation streak, and practice busting out of my shy shell, but after getting groped by him, I regret coming at all.

Three songs play before Johnny makes his way back to our table, but he doesn't sit down. He hands me my beer and takes a chug of his own before leaning in. "Waited so damn long, I drank my beer. I'm going to get another and see if we can't get someone to clean off this table."

I frown at him, confused why he didn't get a beer for himself when he ordered one for me, but I don't question him and simply nod. He angles his head and leans down with his lips puckered, but I quickly grab my beer and bring it to my mouth. No way will his lips touch mine, especially after the butt squeeze.

Stunned, he blinks at me then pecks my cheek before turning his head and looking over his shoulder. There is something odd about his behavior, and I look around him to see where he's looking. The bar isn't as busy as it was.

"It doesn't look that busy."

"What isn't too busy?"

"The bar." I point with the end of my beer bottle.

"Yeah, I hate leaving you alone, but I need another beer." Johnny smiles and pretends to tuck a strand of hair behind my ear. His touch doesn't spark the kind of reaction Jax's featherlight touch did; in fact, it does the opposite and I resist the urge to pull away. "I'll be right back, sexy."

Is this guy for real? He knows nothing about me, we haven't even had a conversation, but he tries to kiss me and calls me pet names, acting like we have some type of connection.

Johnny saunters off toward the bar, not even giving me a backward glance and I hope drinks mean one or two more and not a night of drinking and avoiding his advances. I'm not a confrontational person—I won't tell Johnny his behavior is toeing the line of impropriety—but I will leave.

Several songs play while I sit alone, almost finished with my second beer. Anxiety builds in the pit of my stomach and an uneasy feeling like I'm being watched tickles the back of my neck. I've lost sight of Johnny as more people show up, crowding around the bar and tables.

"Fancy meeting you here." Jax's voice rumbles close to my ear, turning the pit of anxiety into excited butterflies. His featherlight touch against the shell of my ear soothes my tension and I want to relax into his chest. "What's a girl like you doing in a place like this?"

"You… you shouldn't sneak up on a girl like that." I look over my shoulder at him.

"If you saw me, you would have run in the opposite direction." He chuckles and steps around me, then he sits down, scooting his chair close so we can talk without shouting at each other.

"It's always safer to run in the opposite direction of you," I fire back with a smile, bringing my beer bottle to my lips and draining it.

"Thought you might need a refill." Jax smiles back and holds up a beer I didn't notice he was holding. He has two and places one of them in front of me. "What are you doing here?"

"I'm on a date." I bite my lip, eyeing the beer and debating whether I should accept it. Even if I was ready to call it quits with Johnny, accepting a beer from Jax feels wrong.

"Another one?" Jax's arches a brow at me.

I glare at him. "You sound like my brother."

"Now that's just mean." He laughs and brings his beer bottle to his lips, and I can't help but rake my eyes over him. In a Henley shirt and jeans, Jax can make casual look irresistible.

Look, but no touching.

"Jax, I'm surprised to see you here. Aren't you opening a bar?" Johnny pulls my attention away from Jax. I didn't even notice he walked up to our table.

"Johnny." Jax nods at him before flashing a knowing smile at me. "What brings you here?"

"I'm on a date with Hazel." So, it is a date. Johnny wraps an arm around my shoulders and pulls me into his side.

"Oh, is that right?" Jax says, running a hand down his beard and staring Johnny down. I wonder if the two have something against each other.

"Yep." Johnny stiffens when Jax stands from his chair. He's several inches taller than Johnny, his broad shoulders wider, with more lean muscle.

"You shouldn't leave a beautiful woman sitting alone," Jax warns, and Johnny loosens his hold on my shoulders and nods. Disappointment turn my butterflies into lead when I watch Jax disappear into the crowd. I want to follow him, but I turn to face Johnny instead.

"I'm ready to leave." I stand from my chair.

"So soon?" Johnny frowns, tucking his hands into his back pockets. "We haven't even danced yet."

"I'm not dancing," I blurt out, eyeing the fast-moving line dance going on to a song better suited for a club than a country music bar.

"Why not?"

"I don't know how." I turn my attention back to him. "And I'm in heels. Have you seen that dance floor? It's covered in beer and who knows what else. I'll slip and break an ankle."

"I thought you'd be more fun than this." Johnny frowns, pulling his phone out and looking at the screen.

"Sorry to disappoint," I grumble while he taps at his phone before looking back at the bar.

"I need to take care of the tab before we go." He thumbs toward the bar and walks away, not waiting for my response.

This is definitely not the worst date I've been on. Leo will forever be the reigning champ of that title, but this is a close second. Do I smell of desperation that only bottom-barrel men want to ask me out?

I watch Johnny as he leans over the bar to talk with a bartender, who glances at me with a glare that could freeze hell, and I quickly look away, startled by her frostiness. After I wait several seconds, I look back up at Johnny, only he's disappearing behind the bar, the glaring bartender following him.

"Well, great," I murmur to myself, and plop back down in my seat, grabbing the beer Jax gave me, and take a big gulp before slamming it down. If Johnny wants to take off with another woman fine, I can take off, too.

I struggle to make my way to the exit now that more people have packed themselves inside *The Two Step*, and no one seems to care that I'm trying to make my way through them, when a hand wraps around my elbow.

"Follow me." Jax pulls me into his side and navigates us through the throng of people and out the exit and into the cool evening air. The door slams shut behind us, dulling the loud music and heightening my awareness at being alone in a dark parking lot with Jax.

"Thank you." I let out the breath I didn't realize I was holding.

"Where's Johnny?"

"I don't know," I groan and unzip my purse to fish out my phone. I'm going to have to call my brother for a ride or get an Uber.

"Do you need a ride?" Jax reads my mind.

"Yes." I nod and open the Uber app before Jax takes my phone and grabs my hand. "Hey, I need my phone."

"I'll take you home."

"Last time you took me home, you held me hostage."

"Are you always this dramatic?"

"No." I tug on my hand, but he holds it tight while we make our way to his truck.

"So only with me, then?"

"Well, you do have a nasty habit of showing up and ruining my dates."

"I don't ruin your dates. Your dates ruin themselves all on their own." Jax stops and spins around to face me. "What the hell were you doing with Johnny Davidson?"

"I was having… well, we were supposed to have drinks together."

"And he brought you here?" Jax points at *The Two Step*. "Where his ex works? You thought that was a good idea?"

"I didn't know his ex worked here." I look over at *The Two Step*, remembering the bartender who glared at me. "Was it the bartender?"

"Yes." Jax unclenches his jaw and leads me to his truck, opening the passenger door and offering me his hand to help me up.

I don't take it right away but bite my lip before saying, "I didn't know. If I had, I wouldn't have accepted or came here."

Jax places his open hand on his truck and leans in close. "I know."

"Then why are you mad at me?"

"I'm not mad at you. I'm pissed off at Johnny for using you."

"Oh." I lick my lips. I can't see his eyes in the darkness, but the intensity of his stare can be felt, and I melt against his truck.

"Why all the dates?" he asks, moving closer, spiking my heart rate and making it difficult to breathe.

"I… I'm trying to find the one."

"Trying to find the one?" he growls.

I flinch at the anger in his voice and swallow hard before answering, "Yes… is that so hard to believe?"

"No, I just don't get why you keep chasing after guys who don't treat you the way you deserve." That was unexpected, especially coming from Jax. He's been a serial one-night stand kind of guy.

"Why do you care?"

"Why do I care?" Jax asks, as if asking himself the same question. We stand close together in tense silence, neither knowing what to say.

Jax is first to move, bracing his other hand on the other side of his truck, caging me in. Not an inch of space between us and his head descends. The warmth of his breath fans over my face and I lift my chin, ready to meet him, ready to feel his lips against mine. I've wanted to be kissed by Jax since I was a teenage girl and now I have my opportunity, only I don't let it happen. I duck my head against his cheek and groan. If only I had more to drink. I could've let him kiss me and justify it by being drunk, but I didn't drink that much, and I know kissing him will be a mistake. "We can't."

"Why?"

"Because you're my client now." I look up at him, then offer an ultimatum that will ensure he doesn't try anything with me ever again. "You can either kiss me or hire me. You can't have it both ways." I don't like ultimatums, and I do feel a little guilty resorting to such tactics, but he needs a graphic artist more than he wants to kiss me.

"I'll kiss you." Jax's hand wraps around the back of my neck, the other around my waist, and he pulls me into his chest. His mouth slams against mine, obliterating all rational thought, and my arms automatically wrap around his neck, pulling him closer. This isn't a tentative kiss, but one full of passion. Passion that tastes like a dream come true and a happily ever after melted into a delicious treat that I will forever crave.

I don't know who breaks away first, but we are both panting, clutching each other, and one of my legs is wrapped around his. The heat of the moment fades faster than the fog when the sun rises, and I push Jax away.

I bring a hand to my swollen lips. "We can never do that again."

"Why not?"

"Because."

"That isn't an answer."

"But it's the only answer you're going to get."

"I really wish you would tell me what is going on in that pretty little head of yours."

"Can you please just take me home?"

"Not until I get some answers. You give me an ultimatum and when I make my decision, you change your mind. You avoid me, yet you stare at me as if you can't wait to get me naked. What the hell do you want, Hazel, because it's driving me crazy not knowing."

"I don't look at you that way," I lie, crossing my arms over my chest, not out of defiance but to hold myself together.

"You do." He steps back into my personal space. "Either you want me or you don't, which is it?"

"Can it be both?"

"Only if you explain how it's both."

"I'm thinking you are a one and done kind of guy, and I'm not exactly that kind of girl," I tell him honestly, clutching my arms tight, wanting the ground to gobble me up. I might be a shy person, but honesty is important to me and if I expect others to be honest with me, then I have to show them the same courtesy, even when it hurts.

"I see." Jax clenches his jaw and looks away.

"Am I wrong?"

"Get in the truck, I'll take you home." Jax steps away, taking his warmth as he storms to the other side of his truck.

Now I know without a doubt I wasn't wrong. Jax isn't boyfriend material.

I just wish I knew that before he kissed me.

Picture Forever

8

~ Jax ~

Fucking hell, she's under my skin. She thinks she knows me, and she's as stubborn as her brother when she forms an opinion. The air in my truck is stifling with hot tension.

"I'm not who you think I am," I blurt out, clenching the steering wheel when we hit the Peak Valley city limits.

"Excuse me?"

"What you said about me being a one and done kind of guy, that isn't me."

"Oh," she whispers, clasping her hands in her lap, making me more frustrated. Just because I haven't been in a relationship before doesn't make me anti-relationships.

"Oh?" I challenge, not taking my eyes off the road.

"I don't know what to say." I appreciate her honestly, even if it is infuriating, but she isn't telling me what she's thinking, either.

"I want to take you out on a date."

"A date?"

"Yes, a date." I glance at her briefly as I slow my speed as we get closer to her house. I want an answer before I drop her off, and I will drive around the block if she tries to evade me.

"What kind of date?"

"What do you mean, what kind of date? Isn't there only one kind of date?"

"What does a date mean to you?"

"Do you always answer a question with a question?"

"Only when I'm trying to understand what you're after."

"I'm after a date with you. I want to get to know you but mostly, I want *you* to get to know me."

"Okay." She nods, her fingers brushing up against her lips I had the pleasure of tasting and still taste. It was mind-blowing; it surprised me and shifted my world on its axis. She's been driving me crazy, but now she'll drive me insane if I can't have another taste.

"Can I take you out tomorrow?"

"Three dates in three days…"

"Thirds a charm." I try to ease the tension that hasn't quite escaped the cab.

"Fine, but I'm driving myself. I've learned my lesson."

"Whatever you say, Hazel," I say, pulling into her driveway, the tension in my shoulders relaxing as I put my truck into park.

She places a hand on my arm. "Don't walk me up to my door."

I look down at where her hand is touching me. "Why not?"

"Because you'll kiss me when we get there."

"So?"

"So, I think one is enough for tonight."

"Just this once." I smile at her. "But I'm not leaving until you're inside."

"Fair enough." She smiles and exits my truck. I watch her make her way to the front door of her house, glancing back at me every few seconds to see if I'm still here.

I want to jump from this truck and steal a kiss from her, but I restrain myself, unlike I was able to when she gave me the ultimatum. I went for what I wanted, not what I needed, but I don't regret that for a minute. I may never have been a boyfriend before, but that doesn't mean I don't want to be. I never expected Hazel to come along and make me wonder if I could have what my brothers have. Hell, I don't know if I can give her what my brothers are able to give their wives, but I know I want to try.

*****

"Is this another one of your tricks?" Hazel asks when I meet her at the entrance of *Colson Brewery*. She's wearing another sundress, a lavender floral print one with a matching sweater and silver sandals. Her hair is down around her face in glossy waves that make my hands itch, wanting to run my fingers through it, remembering how soft it felt last night.

"No trick." I lead her to where I had set up a table from Dawn, who also helped me set it up for a romantic dinner, complete with candles and flowers. I'm not afraid to enlist my sister-in-law's help. I'm going to need all the help I can get navigating the dating waters.

"So, you have no ulterior motives bringing me here?"

"I want you to get to know me. What better way than to see what I'm trying to build."

"And trick me into taking you on as a client?"

"Such a cynic." I take her hand and squeeze it before pulling her toward her chair. "You really are related to McKnight."

"I'm not a cynic." She glares at me but takes a seat.

"If you want me to take you out to dinner like any other guy I can, but I wanted you to get to know me. You liked my pizza, but you didn't get a chance to enjoy it. Now you can, and I can tell you everything you want to know about me, and you can tell me all about you."

"Your pizza was really good." She eyes the pizza I just pulled from the oven. "And I did like the watermelon beer you made."

"I made sure to have enough Melon Choly Ale just for you." I point to a pail of ice and several bottles of my beer.

"Thank you, Jax," she says with her innocent smile that brightens her brown eyes.

I take a seat across from her. "Should I help you or do you want to dig in?"

"I can handle it," she says and pulls apart the pizza, placing a slice on her plate. "It smells better than I remember."

"It's all about the dough."

I crack open a couple Melon Choly Ales for us as she takes a bite, a soft moan escaping her lips. "It's better than I remembered. I never pictured you a chef."

"I had some help, but making pizza when you have the right ingredients and the perfect dough recipe is easy to make."

"So why a brewery?" she asks, covering her mouth as she chews.

"I spent a lot of time traveling, seeing the world, picking up jobs where I could, but none of the jobs I picked up really mattered to me. I just wanted to get the job done, get paid, and move on.

When I took a job working at a brewery in Colorado, I liked what I did. I never thought I would be the kind of guy who liked working a job, doing the same thing day after day, but I didn't mind work and stayed there longer than I have any other job. I learned a lot and thought I would try my hand at it. After a while, I moved on to another brewery so I could get more insight into the business, and then one day I just decided I was going to start my own brewery someday. It wasn't until I heard Benny planned to sell this place did I really kick-start my plan."

"And now you're here." She smiles, reaching for another slice of pizza.

"And now I'm here." I pick up my slice. "What about you?"

"I went to college, got an internship at a graphic design firm in Kansas City, they later hired me, but then I moved back and started my own graphic design business. Now I'm here."

"Why did you move back to Peak Valley?"

Hazel hesitates for a moment before wiping her mouth with her napkin. "My mom isn't well. She was diagnosed with Alzheimer's not that long ago, and I wanted to spend as much time with her before she…"

"She doesn't remember you," I finish the sentence for her. Hazel nods and looks down at her pizza. "At least you still have your mom. Enjoy the time you have with her."

Hazel looks up at me, her eyes filled with sorrow. "Do you miss your mom?"

"It's hard to miss someone you can't remember."

"I'm sorry, Jax." She reaches for my hand and squeezes it.

I flip my hand and curl my fingers around hers. "Have you always been into graphic design?"

"No, in high school I liked to paint. I thought I would become a painter, but when I was in college, I took a graphic design course and fell in love with digital art. I could turn my sketches and doodles into digital masterpieces and never stopped."

"You still sketch?"

"I do."

"So, how did you get into photography?"

"I stumbled into that. I was working on a website for a company that had a beautiful garden area for its employees. I thought it would be perfect on the website to showcase how they cared about their employees as much as they cared for their customers. I didn't know what I was doing, and I was on a budget, so I borrowed a camera from the firm I worked for and took the shots myself. I've come a long way since then, but it opened up a lot of possibilities when I work with a client."

"You're good with a camera and an amazing graphic designer. I saw the work you've done."

"You have?"

"I did my research…" I wink at her.

"You surprise me, Jax." She smiles and picks up her beer, leaning back in the chair, getting comfortable.

"I hope you mean that as a compliment."

"I do." She nods, then laughs. "Did you know I was one of the painters you modeled for?"

"In high school?" I vaguely remember being a model. I did a lot of things in high school on an impulsive whim, and most of my impulsive whims landed me in trouble.

"You were supposed to just wear regular clothes to the class to model for us. But you showed up wearing a Speedo."

"That's right." I snap my fingers. "Mrs. Jensen didn't care, but Principal Carter did. I got two days in-school suspension for that. Is that why you've been trying to avoid me? Because I wore a

Speedo to your art class? Or do you really think I'm… what was it you said? One and done?"

"It isn't because of the Speedo. I tried to avoid you because I remember what you were like in high school."

"And how was I in high school?"

"You changed girls faster than you changed your clothes."

"I think you are being a little dramatic."

"I think you—"

"Hazel?" McKnight yells, storming through the front door. "What the *hell* are you doing here?"

"Warren, what are *you* doing here?" She really does like to answer a question with a question, even with her brother.

"One of my deputies saw your car here."

"And you decided to pay a little visit?" I lean back and fold my arms across my chest. "We were enjoying a lovely dinner before you barged in."

"Is this a date?" McKnight waves his finger around the table.

"Yes, and you're ruining it." I smirk, knowing annoying McKnight won't get him to leave anytime soon but unable to help myself.

McKnight looks at Hazel with narrowed eyes. "I thought you said he wasn't your type."

"Oh, she made me aware of that." I flash a teasing grin at Hazel.

McKnight fisting his hands, agitated. "C'mon, Hazel, I'll follow you home."

"Excuse me?" Hazel looks stunned at her brother. "You can't order me around like that."

"I can when it means protecting you."

"Protecting her from who? Me?" I throw my napkin onto the table. "What the hell do you think is going to happen."

"Nothing, because this," McKnight points at us both, "isn't going to happen." Then he turns so his back is facing me and lowers his voice. "I know you promised Mom you would try to settle down and get married before she gets too sick, but you're not being smart about it."

"Too far, McKnight." I stand and put a hand on his shoulder. I don't know what promise he's talking about, but I do know that he shouldn't talk to his sister that way. She's a grown woman who can speak for herself. "Stop bossing her around and let her make her own decisions."

McKnight looks down at my hand, then back at me. "Do you mind removing that hand?"

I remove my hand. I'm not interested in starting a fight with McKnight, but I don't like the way he's ordering Hazel around, nor do I like the assumptions he's making, even if they were formed based on my past behavior. It doesn't mean I haven't changed.

"Warren, I think you're overreacting. It's one date." Hazel takes the napkin from her lap and places it on the table before standing.

McKnight pinches the bridge of his nose, letting out a groan of stress. "Fine, do what you want." He sighs then faces me. "Make sure she gets home safe." Then he faces Hazel. "Call me when you get home and make sure all the windows and doors are locked. I'll have a deputy patrol your house."

"Why are you on high alert? I would never let anything happen to Hazel," I demand.

"Does the term 'eye for an eye' ring any bells?" He ignores me, shifting his attention to Hazel.

"No why?" She scrunches her nose and looks at me with confusion.

"Has anyone said it to you? Mentioned it in passing?"

"No."

"Is she in some kind of danger?"

"No, but I'm not taking any chances." McKnight faces me again, placing a hand on the back of his neck and rolling his head. "There's been a murder. I can't get into the details, but I think its best if everyone takes precautions."

"Murder?" Hazel covers her mouth with her hands then whispers, "Who was murdered?"

"Kevin Hunt's wife."

"Kevin Hunt, Peak Valley's District Attorney?" I ask, running a hand over my beard. I can see why McKnight is concerned. He's known for putting bad guys in jail and throwing away the key. He's likely to have a lot of enemies… enemies who want revenge.

"Yes." McKnight gives me a knowing look. He's worried, but what does Kevin's wife being murdered have to do with Hazel, where he had to track her down and make sure she's okay?

"Do you have any suspects?"

"Not at this time, and I ask that you keep this to yourselves. The town will know soon enough. I need to focus on catching the person before the town begins to panic."

"I'll make sure she gets home safe."

"I appreciate that, but that isn't a free pass. If you're going to date my sister, I expect you to respect her or *this*," he waves his hand around my brewery, "will never happen. I'll make sure you never open."

"Warren…"

"I don't care if you're Eric's brother; she's my sister and deserves to be treated like a princess."

"I'm not a princess, Warren. I'm an adult and I know what I deserve, and it isn't you coming in here and being bossy." Hazel lifts her chin, and I'm proud of her for speaking up to her brother.

"You know what I mean." McKnight briefly shuts his eyes and shakes his head. "I need to get going. Keep your guard up." He puts a finger under Hazel's chin and tilts it so she is looking in his eyes. "Promise me you'll be cautious."

Worry fills her eyes and little stress lines crease at her forehead. "I promise."

McKnight looks at me, releasing Hazel's chin and jabbing a finger into my chest. "I'll be seeing you. Soon."

I raise my arms with a smirk. "You know where to find me."

McKnight jabs again. "I'm telling your brother."

"He already knows. Or kind of knows," Hazel adds, shrugging her shoulders. "He didn't want to get into it. But I don't think he knows about this date. Not that the other night was a date, or when you took me home last night." Hazel's eyes widen and she slams a hand over her mouth, cutting off her rambling.

"What happened last night?"

"I came to her rescue." I laugh. "Again."

"Again?" McKnight growls at Hazel. "What the hell, Hazel?"

"I was going to call you or an Uber, but Jax sort of kidnapped me."

"I didn't kidnap you," I groan and let my head fall back. "Don't be so dramatic."

"Don't count on that ever happening."

"Hey!" Hazel smacks McKnight in the shoulder. "I'm not dramatic."

"You are." McKnight arches an eyebrow. "Sunday, you'll tell me everything or I'm going to have him," McKnight thumbs at me, "tell me everything."

"Ugh, whatever." Hazel rolls her eyes and waves McKnight away. "You can go now."

McKnight gives me a warning looking. "Behave."

"I'll be on my best behavior." I flash my full-watt smile and wiggle my eyebrows.

"Son of bitch," McKnight swears as he leaves.

"You just can't help yourself, can you?" Hazel folds her arms on the table with a playful smile.

"Help myself how?"

"You always have to stir the pot, don't you?" She smiles. "It's your kryptonite. If you can cause mischief, you will."

"I'm an opportunist. If I see an opportunity, I'm taking it."

"And if you see an opportunity to trick me, will you?"

"Depends?"

"On what?"

"On whether I can trick a kiss out of you."

*****

"You don't have to follow me or walk me to the door." Hazel nibbles on her bottom lip.

"What kind of gentlemen would I be if I don't? Besides, I need to check the house," I say, meeting her halfway up her driveway.

"Check the house?" Her brows dart together in confusion.

"Make sure all the windows are locked and the house is secure."

"I can do that," she says, fidgeting with the buttons on her sweater.

"I know you can, but for peace of mind, I intend to do it as well." I wink and wrap a hand around her waist and lead her up the path to her front porch.

"I really had a good time; thank you for making me dinner. The pizza was delicious."

"I'm glad you liked it." I smile at her adorable rambling and lean against the frame of the door, watching her nervous fingers try to unlock it. "Need some help?"

"Nope. I've got it." She shakes her head, wiggling the key into the lock on the third try.

"Am I making you nervous?"

"Yes." She opens the door and flips on the lights as she walks in. "Very nervous."

"Dramatic and honest, I like that." I step in and look around.

"I'm not dramatic," she grumbles, putting her purse down on the table leading into a small living room.

Her house is a small starter home, with two bedrooms and one bathroom, and just the right size for her. The living room is a colorful array of digital artwork, pottery, and glass-blown sculptures. If there wasn't a couch and a TV, the room could be staged as an art gallery. Her personality shines through the décor, as if giving a little glimpse into what makes her tick.

"I like all the art. Is it yours?"

"Some of it…" She looks around at the different pieces sprinkled around the room with a shy smile.

"Want to show me around?"

"Show you around?"

"Show me your house, tell me about your art. I'll check the windows and secure the house as we go."

"You want to know about the art?" She continues to nibble on her lip.

I step into her personal space and tug gently on her lip with my thumb before running my knuckles against her cheek. "I want to know about your art, and everything else that makes you, you."

Hazel sways on her feet but doesn't move or say anything. Our eyes lock and she licks her lips as my fingers slide down and curl around her neck, pulling her closer to me. "I'm not having sex with you," she blurts, and I pause my pursuit.

"Okay…?" I tilt my head to the side. "Is kissing off the table, too?"

"No… I mean *yes*." She tries to step back, but I don't let her move, fisting her hair and molding her body against mine.

"Are you sure about that?"

"Not at all," she breathes out and I capitalize on her hesitancy, laying my mouth over hers in a gentle caress to chase away her reluctance. I may be new to being a boyfriend, but I know how to kiss her, and she knows how to kiss me. It's a new experience—kissing a woman with the desire to keep on kissing her until she won't let me anymore. I love it, crave it, and I want more of it.

Her tits press against my chest and my hand moves from her hip to the lower part of her back, wanting to feel her skin, caress it, and taste it, but her sundress serves as a barrier. My dick grows twice its size pressing into her lower belly, and her breath catches before she rips her mouth from mine and moans. "We have to stop."

"Why?" I demand, squeezing her tight against my body, feeling her soft parts against all my hard parts only makes my dick twitch, and she squirms in my arms.

"Because…" She leans her forehead against my chest, hiding her face and the blush she undoubtably has on her face. She blushes a lot, especially when she's staring at me, and it drives me wild wanting to know if that blush flushes her entire body.

"That isn't an answer."

"Well, it's the only answer you're going to get," she mumbles into my chest.

"So stubborn." I chuckle, kissing the shell of her ear, smiling when she shivers in my arms.

"I'm not stubborn, I'm being… practical."

"Still worried I'm only after one thing?" I lean back and tilt her head so I can see her beautiful brown eyes.

"Yes… I mean no. Can we take it slow?" She bites that lower lip of hers.

"I can do slow." *At least, I think I can.*

Her smile knocks me off-kilter. She brightens a room with an innocence that pushes all your troubles away and warms your soul. It draws out a protective side in me I've never felt for a woman before.

9

~ Hazel ~

Sunday morning sunshine filters into my room, waking me up with a smile on my face. Dreams of Jax kissing and worshipping my body replay like happy memories as I stretch beneath my sheets.

I want to be wrong about it. I want him to be boyfriend material, but it's too soon to tell and I don't want to get my hopes up only to be let down. Not letting my hopes get the better of me is going to be a problem, especially if he keeps kissing me like he did last night and at *The Two Step*.

There is more to him than just his kissing abilities, too. He's come a long way since high school. No longer is he the boy who plays pranks; he's a man who is starting a business and who cares about my safety and is interested in my art.

My alarm beeps at my bedside table, reminding me I need to get up and around so I can take my mother to get her hair done today. The retirement community has a woman come in providing hair and nail services, but I wanted to get her out of the retirement community and see the town again. I worry her self-imposed isolation will cause her to accelerate the inevitable, and I'm determined not to let that happen

I quickly run through my morning routine, throwing on a pair of yoga pants, a tank top, and a chunky oversized sweater. The wind has a bit of a chill and soon I'll have to pack away my summer dresses for Uggs and sweaters.

I don't bother with makeup and throw my hair into a messy bun before grabbing my purse and move out the door.

"You're in a happy mood," my mom notes when we pull into the salon parking lot.

"I am." I nod, putting my car into park. "Aren't you?"

"I suppose so, but you're in a good mood like you got laid last night."

"Mom!"

"What? Did you?"

"No, and I'm not talking about sex with you," I cry out, opening my car door.

"Why not?" She pulls herself out of my car. "Your twenty-seven years old, you shouldn't be worried about what I think when it comes to sex. Besides, I think it'll be good for you."

"You think me getting laid would be good for me?" I give her a skeptical glance over the top of my car.

"Getting laid is good for everyone. I'd be in a better mood if I was getting laid."

"I don't want to hear that!"

"Sheesh, such a prude. Maybe that's why you're still single," Mom huffs and walks toward the salon. "Coming?"

"I need more coffee," I groan, catching up with her.

"I heard you went out on a date with Leo Waugh. How did that go?"

"Terrible." I close my eyes, not wanting to hear the latest gossip concerning me and Leo.

"Good, his mother is *dreadful*," my mother whispers. "Never shuts up about that son of hers."

"Oh, I know." I laugh. "She wouldn't shut up about him during our date."

"No!" My mom covers her mouth in disbelief. "She went on the date with you?"

"Yep."

Mom shrugs open the salon door. "Well, I guess I'm not all that surprised. He took his mother with him on a date with Melissa what's-her-name who used to live down the street from us."

"Oh, good Lord, this wasn't his first time?"

"I doubt it be the last, either," Mom whispers when Cat, Mom's stylist, comes to greet up. Cat gets my mom seated in a chair and talks to her about what she wants done to her hair.

"Do you mind if I pop over to get some coffee at *Sugar n' Sweet*?" I ask as Cat is snapping a cape over Mom.

"Sure." Cat smiles at me through the mirror.

"Are you okay with me going, Mom?"

"Go, I'll be fine, Hazel." My mom waves me off.

"Okay, I'm going. Do you want anything?"

"No, I'm fine."

"Okay. I'll be right back."

The whole town must be in line for a cup of coffee at *Sugar n' Sweet* when I arrive. After waiting for fifteen minutes, I'm ready to head back, not wanting to leave my mom alone for too long, but I'm close to the front of the line and decide to stay when my phone rings and unfamiliar number scrolls across the screen. Not wanting to disrupt the people around me nor carry on a conversation I may not want the town of Peak Valley to be privy to, I silence my phone and tuck it back into my purse.

It takes another ten minutes to get my coffee and a brownie for my mom before I'm out the door, heading back to the salon with a little skip in my step.

Before I reach the door, Cat throws it open. "I've been trying to call you."

"Oh sorry, I wasn't—"

"Your mom… she ran out of here about fifteen minutes ago."

"Ran out?"

"She was mumbling something I couldn't understand and wouldn't sit still. I offered to get her a glass of water and when I came back, she was gone."

"Gone?" I ask, gripping my coffee cup so I don't drop it as the pounding of my heart roars in my ears.

"I'm sorry. I looked up and down the street for her but haven't found her. What should I do?"

"Can you call my brother, Sherriff Warren McKnight?"

"Yes." She nods, wringing her hands on the verge of tears.

"It's okay, Cat," I try to reassure her. "It isn't your fault. I should have told you my mom has Alzheimer's. Please, if you could call my brother, I'll go look for her."

Her face turns white. "Alzheimer's?"

"Please go call my brother, I'm going to look for her." I turn on my heel and head for my car. I have a better chance at finding her if I can cover more ground.

My heart feels like it's about to pound out of my chest, and I fight the urge to cry. Now is not the time to panic. I need to focus and search for my mom. I can fall apart after I find her.

"What was I thinking!" I slam my car door shut, laying my head against the steering wheel when a knock on my window scares the ever-living daylights out of me.

"Hazel, you, okay?" Jax taps on the window, then opens my car door. "What's going on? You tore off down Main Street and must not have heard me calling your name."

Jax! "My mom. She ran off and is wandering the streets. I have to find her before something horrible happens to her."

Jax presses his lips together and scans over the parking lot. "Get out."

"What?"

"Get out of the car, I'll drive while you look for your mom."

"Okay, yes, yes… that's a good idea. I can try to call my brother." I unfold from my car and stop when Jax wraps a hand around the back of my neck.

"It'll be okay. We'll find her," he whispers, pulling me for a quick hug and briefly kisses my forehead. My heart slows its pace, comforted by Jax and his willingness to stop everything to help me.

We're on the main street heading south toward the Peak Valley Retirement Community when my phone rings and my brother's name appears across the display.

"Warren, I'm so sorry. I should have never left her alone." I drop my head in shame.

"Take a deep breath, Hazel. No one could have expected this. I have all my deputies looking for her. We'll find her," he reassures me, but it brings little comfort. Jax lays a hand on my thigh and squeezes before making a U-turn and heads back toward the center of town. "Where are you now?"

"Um, heading back toward the center of town."

"I'm going to head toward your old house," Jax chimes in.

"Who is that?" Warren demands.

"Jax. He's heading toward our old house."

"Good idea," Warren says. "Call me back if you find her."

"You do the same." I nod as if he can see me and hang up.

"What is she wearing?" Jax asks, releasing my thigh and pulling his phone out of his pocket.

"Um… a lavender cardigan and jeans."

Jax has his phone to his ear. "I need a favor. Are you at work?" I can't hear whoever is on the other end of the phone. "I'm with Hazel and we're looking for her mom. If a woman comes in with a lavender cardigan and jeans, can you call me? She has Alzheimer's." His conversation makes my heart lurch and my stomach to bottom out. "Thanks."

"Who was that?"

"Amber." Jax side-eyes me before turning down my old street. "She'll call if your mom is brought into the hospital."

Hospital? "Oh…" I swallow and look out the window, searching the street for any sign of my mom as my vision begins to blur with tears I've desperately tried to hold back when I spot my mom. "Stop the car!"

"Do you see her?"

"Yes, she's sitting on our old front porch."

Jax pulls the car over, parking in front of my childhood home, and I'm out of the car before it comes to a stop and dialing my brother.

"Did you find her?"

"Yes, she's at the old house."

"I'm on my way." I hang up and tuck my phone into my back pocket, running up the stairs where my mom is sitting on the bench swing my father installed for her more than fifteen years ago.

"Mom!"

"Hazel, well, this is a surprise. Come have a seat with me." My mom pats the empty seat next to her, still wearing the stylist's cape.

"I've been looking all over for you." I take a shaky a breath and lean forward, pulling her into a tight hug as I take a seat next to her.

She runs a hand down my hair. "I've been right here."

The doctor warned me that in moments of unclarity, it's best not to upset her, especially when she is in a place where medical care can't easily be provided. I release her from the hug, taking her hand and lean back while she starts to hum to herself. Jax comes up the steps, as the front door opens and a young mother holding her baby on her hip peers through the screen door at us. Jax softly explains the situation to her, and I'm grateful he's here. The woman gives me a sympathetic smile and tells Jax to take our time before she quietly shuts the door.

Warren arrives only a few minutes later and climbs the steps with a grim look on his face.

"Warren?" Mom squints her eyes at him, then looks down at the cape still draped over her. "Where am I?"

"You're at the old house." I squeeze her hand.

"How did I get here?" She looks at me, then at Warren, before her eyes land on Jax. "Who are you?"

"Jax Colson." Jax steps forward.

"Oh, you're Elizabeth's youngest boy." My mom stands. "Come here and give me a hug I haven't seen you since her funeral."

"You knew my mom?" Jax asks, hesitating before walking into her embrace.

"She was my dearest friend." She squeezes him. "And I miss her terribly."

"Mom?" I stand and wrap an arm around her shoulders. "We should get you back home."

"Yes, yes, we have dinner to prepare."

"I'll follow you." Warren tips his head at us and I lead my mom toward my car, Jax at my side.

"What am I wearing?" She plucks at the cape. "Is this a poncho? Was it supposed to rain?"

"No, Mom, we can take it off." I unsnap the buttons at the back and scrunch the cape in my arms. Jax takes it from me and opens the backseat door.

"Are you going to stay for dinner?" Mom asks Jax, placing a hand on his cheek.

"If you'll have me…" Jax flashes a sweet smile at her and my heart skips a beat.

"Oh, wonderful. I want to hear all about your shenanigans. You were always such a wild little thing."

*****

Warren helps my mother into her apartment, but I linger behind. I need a moment to myself before I walk in and pretend nothing serious happened. Warren and I have to talk about future plans for Mom. We've put it off for too long, but I can't talk about it today. Not after witnessing first-hand the devastation Alzheimer's disease causes.

"You okay?" Jax asks, standing next to me with nothing but tenderness in his eyes, which causes tears to blur my vision and a lump to form in my throat. His arms wrap around me, sensing the impeding breakdown, and I sob into his chest. Big fat tears roll down my cheeks, soaking his shirt while he rubs my back. He doesn't say anything, just holds me. I have never been so grateful to have someone there by my side weathering the storm.

My tears seemed endless and still, Jax holds me, his arms like a warm blanket I don't want to emerge from, but I can't hide within his embrace, no matter how wonderful it feels. I can't avoid going inside, not when Sunday dinner is going to play out as if nothing ever happened.

"We should get inside," I sniffle into Jax's chest.

"Take all the time you need; your brother can help your mom for a little while." Jax tilts my chin up, wiping away a tear with his thumb.

"I'm sorry I ruined your Sunday," I whisper as another wave of tears threatens to spill over.

"You didn't ruin my Sunday. I'm glad we found your mom, and she's safe." He stares deep into my eyes. I have wanted to kiss Jax, my high school crush, since the moment I saw him, but in this tender moment, I want to kiss the man who helped me in my darkest hour. He didn't run. He didn't shy away from my mom and her failing memory; he stood by me, helped me. His genuine kindness penetrated my insecurities and my barriers that I put up to protect me from him, and he stole my heart. I'm in more danger of being utterly and completely devastated by the charming trickster than I ever was before.

Picture Forever

10

~ Jax ~

"Wait, my mom dated Warren's dad?" I give Maria, Hazel's mom, a skeptical look. "I don't believe you."

"Oh, you rascal." Maria waves her hand at me with a beautiful smile, and it's obvious that Hazel gets her smile from her mother. "They were high school sweethearts until your father came along and whisked her off her feet."

"I never knew that." I scratch my bearded chin and then wiggle my eyebrows at Warren. "We could have been brothers."

"Thank fuck we aren't." McKnight leans back in his chair and smirks at me. Both McKnight and Hazel have been quiet over dinner, picking at their food while their mom chats away, retelling stories that barely bring a smile to Hazel. She was born to smile, and it clenches my gut when her normally bright smile is replaced with a forced one.

"Hey, language." Maria glares at McKnight, and I laugh when his smirk is wiped clean from his face.

"So how did you and Warren Sr. get together?" Hazel asks, pecking at the last of her dinner. It's the first time she's really engaged in the conversation and I'm hopeful she's about to pull herself out of her rut.

"After Elizabeth and Rusty were married, Warren Sr. and I ran into each other at the grocery store. He just started working as a deputy and was quite the charmer." Maria shares a sad look in her eyes. I don't think Warren Sr. was the true charmer she had hoped he would be. I can't picture the man ever being charming. He's been a thorn in my side and cost Luke most of his adulthood without the love of his life. McKnight may be an asshole, but he's nothing compared to his father.

"Is that why Warren Sr. hates my brothers and me so much? Our dad stole my mom from him?"

Maria frowns as sorrow fills her brown eyes before nodding. "That, and he blamed your father for her death."

"But she died in a car accident that my dad wasn't even involved in." My mom was driving home from work when she was killed in a car accident. Our father was home making dinner when someone came to the door to inform him. I was too young and don't remember much after that, but I remember when my dad received the news. I lost my dad that day, too. He turned into a monster as he slowly let his demons devour him.

"I know, dear, but Warren Sr. thought if Elizabeth never met Rusty, she'd still be alive today."

"But Dad was married to you," McKnight points out, letting his chair fall to the ground with a loud thud. We are entering dangerous territory the more Maria shares Warren Sr.'s past, but I don't want to cut it short. Maria is the first person

I've met who really knew my mother before she died. I don't have many memories of her, being so young when she died, so I borrow memories to fill in what I missed out on.

"We were married, and I'm sorry, Warren, but it was also what led to our divorce. I thought he might still be in love with Elizabeth when we first started dating, but I cared about him a lot and hoped it would fade, but over time it didn't and drove a wedge between us."

"Can we change the subject?" McKnight asks, looking uncomfortable. I'd probably be too if I were in his shoes. I wouldn't want to hear about my dad loving another woman who wasn't my mother or his wife. I know what it's like to grow up hearing shameful stories about your father, and I don't wish it on anyone.

"Yes, I know this must be hard for you." Maria pats Warren's hand. "But I think it's important you hear the truth, especially since you and Eric patched things up. You two were thick as thieves when you were little. Did you know Elizabeth was so sure Eric was going to be a girl?" She changes the subject, her eyes bright with excitement. I don't know if her shift is for McKnight's benefit or her Alzheimer's. "She had grand plans for Warren and her baby. She was so sure it was a girl and that they would get married, but then out popped Eric."

I slap my chest and laugh. "Thank you, Maria. I will never let Eric forget that Mom thought he was going to be a girl."

"You're welcome, dear." She winks at me, then sighs and looks around the table. "As fun as this has been, I'm plum tired out and we still need to clean up."

"I'll take care of the dishes," Hazel offers, standing from the table and picking up Maria's plate. Her quiet demeanor isn't new; I've watched her long enough to know she prefers to listen rather than engage, but there's always a brightness to her, a quiet joy that has been missing since I found her in her car on the verge of tears. I'd risk everything, pay whatever the cost, lose my soul if it would give her back her joy, but I can't cure Alzheimer's and I've never felt more helpless.

"I'll help." I stand and carry my plate to the kitchen.

"Thank you." Maria's eyes glow with happiness. "Warren, give me a hand?" Maria holds her hand out for Warren, who clasps it and helps her walk around the table, leading her toward the bedroom.

"You don't have to help," Hazel says when I enter the kitchen.

"I know I don't have to, but I would appreciate it if you'd let me." I set my dishes in the sink and wrap a hand around her neck, pulling her in and kissing her temple.

"Are you sure?" She sighs and some of the tension melts from her shoulders. I like having that kind of effect on her.

"I help with dishes at my family Sunday dinners," I point out. I take a plate she just rinsed and put it inside the dishwasher.

Hazel stops rinsing the dish she's holding and looks up at me wide-eyed. "You missed your Sunday dinner with your family."

I take the plate she's holding. "This is where I'm supposed to be."

"Bullshit," McKnight mutters, coming into the kitchen with his dinner plate and the leftover salad.

"You're just upset you lost your chance at marrying my brother," I throw back.

McKnight punches me hard in the shoulder and I grunt, taking a step back and rubbing my shoulder. "Asshole."

"Warren!" Hazel shoves him. "Out. We'll take care of this mess. Here, take the trash out."

McKnight glares at me while Hazel pulls the trash from the bin and hands it to him. She waits for him to leave before turning to face me. "Did he hurt you?"

"Yes." I wrap a hand around her waist. "I think you need to kiss me and make it feel better."

"And if I don't?" Hazel raises an eyebrow with a just a sliver of brightness in her smile. I pull her into my chest, wanting to coax more out of her.

"I'll whine until you do." My head descends until our lips nearly touch. "Please."

Hazel doesn't wait for me to ask again before she pushes up on her toes and wraps her hands around my neck, fusing us together. My hand traces up her back, fisting her hair and molding us together. I didn't intend for this kiss to be full of passion, but her need to forget the awfulness of the day fuels us both, deepening the kiss until a hand grabs the back of my shirt and hauls me back.

"Get your paws off my sister." McKnight shoves me back and stands between me and Hazel. "Can you not do *that* in my presence?"

"You're being ridiculous." Hazel smacks the back of his head and I laugh, seeing McKnight get knocked around by Hazel. A little more of her brightness shines through.

"I'd say get a room, but you're my sister and I don't want to *think* about you being with this asshole." He rubs the back of his head.

"Grow up, McKnight." I run a hand down my face, rolling my shoulders. His disapproval over Hazel and me dating is starting to get old.

McKnight points a finger at me. "I *will* arrest you."

"We're leaving. *You* can clean this mess up on your own." Hazel throws up her arms and sidesteps around McKnight.

I take Hazel's hand and wave to McKnight, flashing my full-watt smile. "See you around, McKnight."

"Overgrown baby," Hazel mutters, storming out of the apartment. "He didn't care about me dating Leo or Johnny, but the second I kiss you, he goes crazy."

"To be fair, you never kissed Leo or Johnny," I point out, following her fast pursuit to the car.

"That doesn't matter."

"Sure it does."

She turns on me so fast, I nearly plow into her. "How so?"

"Because he knew they weren't going to last."

Hazel's shoulders relax and her face softens as my chest tightens. Her quiet joy isn't fully restored, but it's enough to reassure me I can help her find it. "And you will?"

"That's the goal, isn't it?"

"But we've only been on one date."

"And I want to take you on other dates. I also want to kiss you more."

"So, we're dating?"

"We're dating." I nod, then tilt my head. "What did you think we were doing?

"I… don't know." She flashes a quizzical look. "And are we only dating each other?"

"Yes." I rub the back of my neck. "Are you dating another loser I have to save you from?"

She rolls her eyes. "No."

"Good. So when can I see you again?"

"Um… Wednesday?" She bites her lip. "Unless you want to wait until the weekend."

"Wednesday works for me."

"Wednesday it is." She flashes her bright smile at me, and the world is right again.

*****

Texting with Hazel isn't enough. I need to feel her lips against mine. Taste her innocence and soak it in to feed my soul. She's under my skin, in my head, and warming my heart. I didn't know being a boyfriend could feel so good. I wanted to make time to stop in and see her on Monday, but the brewing barrels arrived, and I spent most of the day and evening getting them installed and taking inventory of the supplies I need before I can start brewing my liquid gold in large quantities.

By the time I got home, it was late and Hazel was in bed. As much as I wanted to drive over to her place and crawl into bed beside her, I knew she'd freak out. Timing is everything when it comes to relationships. At least, that's what Dawn said when she and Clint came over to check on the installation of the barrels.

I woke up refreshed on Tuesday with dreams of Hazel's sun-kissed skin and bright smile. Those images lingered in my head and made my dick throb, and I had to beat off in the shower just to relieve the tension. *I need to see her.* Even if it's only for a few minutes.

Running through my morning routine, I head for *Sugar n' Sweet* for my morning coffee and grab a cup for Hazel, along with a few bagels.

She's sitting behind the lobby desk and doesn't notice me until the chimes over her office door announce my presence. "How do you like your coffee?"

"I like a little bit of cream." She smiles at me and stands from behind the desk, meeting me halfway and planting a quick kiss to my cheek. It isn't close to what I was hoping for. "I wasn't expecting you."

"Am I not allowed to pop in? I thought that's what you get to do when you're dating someone."

"Feel free to pop in whenever you feel the need to caffeinate me." She takes the coffee and leads me to where a small break area is set up just off the lobby.

"I was thinking I would take you to the *Prairie Fed Steak House* in River Bend tomorrow night. You like steak, right?"

"I do," she says, pulling some creamer out of the mini fridge and pouring a little into her coffee.

"Good, I was worried you were going to tell me you were a vegetarian." I pull her close, taking her coffee from her hand and putting it on the counter.

"You've seen me eat meat." Her free hands wrap around my waist. "You put chicken on the pizza you made me."

"Yeah, but not red meat."

"Not eating red meat doesn't make you a vegetarian." She laughs.

I tilt my head, pretending to ponder it. "Are you sure?"

"Yes, you goof." She tries to push me away, but I tighten my grip.

"Mmm." I shrug. "What's your day look like?"

"I'm working on some sketches for your branding."

"You are?" I jerk my head back and scan her face. "I thought you weren't going to do my branding."

"Liar." She laughs again. I love making her laugh. It's a magical melody that the whole world should be allowed to listen to.

"I'd be offended by that if I had low self-esteem." I tickle her side and she lets out a little squeak, squirming from my grip.

She shoves me with a laugh. "Oh, we both know your ego isn't capable of being offended."

"I'd be offended by that as well." I fake a pout. "I deserve a kiss for that."

Hazel doesn't hesitate and closes the small gap between up, pushing up on her toes and meeting me halfway. My hands find her waist, taking their time to feel her soft curves, learning her form, and committing it to memory.

She breaks free from my grip again and steps out of reach. "Oh, no, you don't. I'm working. I can't have you enticing me with your lips."

"So, I entice you?" I smirk at her and try to reel her in for more.

"You know you do." She takes another step out of reach.

"Aren't we supposed to sneak around and make out?"

"Yes, but not while I have work to do."

"Do you get a break?"

"No."

"Who's your boss? I want to have words with them."

"Funny." She rolls her eyes. "Come look at the sketches I've made. I want to know if you like them."

As much as I would love to coax more kisses from Hazel, I know I need to get on my branding. Just learning that she's been working on something for me already sparks my curiosity. "Are you sure you're okay with doing the branding?"

"I was hit with inspiration." She dazzles me with her bright smile. I'd kill for that smile if it wouldn't land me in prison. "I couldn't stop sketching yesterday."

Hazel spreads out several pieces of paper with sketches of various logos. There are so many sketches, she must have spent hours working on them.

"Is that a melon on a dog's head?"

"It's a melon on a *collie*." Hazel laughs, nibbling her thumb nail. "Get it... melon collie."

It's the most ridiculous thing I've heard and exactly what my beer needs. I cover my mouth to hold back the snort. "It's unexpectedly perfect. Fun and fruity, just like my beer."

"That's exactly what I was thinking." She laughs again. "It's one of my favorites."

"Is this a logo for the brewery?" I hold up a sketch with a bearded man who looks a lot like me, posed like Popeye, only fiercer and holding a frosted mug with *Colson Brewery* lettered on it.

"It's one of the logos I sketched. I like it the most."

"I love it." I stare down at the sketch. It's a mixture of whimsical meets masculinity. "This is exactly what I was looking for."

"It is?"

"Yes, and the separate branding for the Melon Choly Ale can tie together with this."

"That's what you wanted, right?"

"It's exactly what I wanted." I grab her waist and pull her into my side. "You're fucking phenomenal."

"Oh please, you're just fishing for a kiss."

"No, I'm serious, Hazel. This is perfect. I can't wait to see the finished product."

"Seriously?"

"Seriously." I couldn't have asked for a better logo. The other artists I went to were good, but they lacked a uniqueness Hazel was able to bring forth. It's a logo that will stand out and capture people's attention. "You're going to help put me on the map."

"Don't be so dramatic." Hazel giggles.

*****

"I like this dress you're wearing," I tell Hazel for probably the tenth time, but I don't care.

She's fucking gorgeous, rocking another little black dress that hugs her curves. I will go to sleep tonight dreaming about her in this dress. It'll be pure, blissful torture.

"You said that already." She giggles as I hold open the door to *Prairie Fed Steak House*.

"Just making sure you know how much I appreciate it."

"You will keep your hands to yourself while we eat," Hazel warns, giving me a pointed stare. "I'm starving."

"I make no promises." I wink at her. "Reservation for two. Colson."

"Okay, just one moment." The hostess scans her finger down until she sees my name. "Table for two. Right this way." She points her hand to the right and leads us through the dimly lit room where other couples and small families are dining. "Here we are. I hope you enjoy your meal."

"Thank you." Hazel smiles at the girl while I pull out her chair. *Thank you, Dawn, for your wonderful wisdom.* She made sure to call me with several tips on how to be a gentleman. I'm choosing not to believe she doubts my abilities.

"Have you been here before?" Hazel asks when I take my seat. She's looking around at the décor, which had surprised me when we first walked in. It's a nice restaurant with crisp white tablecloths, beautiful candle centerpieces, but the walls are covered in pictures of sports teams and sign memorabilia.

"No, but Clint took Dawn here, and she highly recommended it. I'm not a fan of the décor, but if Dawn says the food is good, then you know it's true."

"Dawn seems to be a big influencer in your life."

"She's the sister I never had and can cook. Have you had her lasagna?" I pick up my menu and run through my choices.

"No, I haven't, but I'm not surprised you are easily won over by food," Hazel says.

"Do you want a bottle of wine? I don't have a clue when it comes to wine."

"I'm good with beer."

"You're turning me on, Hazel." I glance at her over the menu with a flirty smile.

"Because I like beer?"

"Because you like beer and you look amazing in that dress."

"You're easy to please."

"I'm an easy man," I say, then frown. "Wait… That came out wrong."

"I think it came out just right," Hazel laughs as are server arrives.

"Hello, I'm Alex, and I'll be your server for the evening. Do you know what you would like to drink, or do you need some more time?"

"Will you order a beer for me?" Hazel asks, looking over her menu.

"Two Imperial Stouts."

"Excellent choice. They go well with our ribeye." Alex nods and leaves us.

"Should I get the ribeye?"

"I am."

"Jax, is that you?" Burns shouts from across the restaurant at the hostess stand. He waves a hand at us. "Jax, over here."

"Oh for the love of all things holy, what the *hell* is that man doing here?" I cringe and wave.

The hostess turns to look at us, saying something to Burns and Miss Janet, only for Burns to ignore her and head for our table. Hazel turns, spotting Burns and Miss Janet, and waves at them.

"Do not encourage him."

"I'm not encouraging him. I'm just waving." Hazel's mouth twitches in a barely concealed smile. If those two were ever to join forces, my life would turn to hell.

"We need two more chairs." Burns marches over to us, waving at the hostess. Crafty bastard must have planned this. "Can we get two more chairs over here?"

"Burns, they don't want to sit with us. They are on a *date*." Miss Janet shakes her head, following him.

"Of course, they want to sit with us." Burns comes to stand next to Hazel. "Nice to see you again, Hazel."

Alex comes over holding our Imperial Stouts. "Would you like to move to a bigger table?"

"Yes, sir, we would." Burns tugs on the lapels of his jacket.

"We have a table right over here." Alex uses his head to point to the booth catacorner from our table.

"We don't have to move, Hazel." I rest my elbow on the table and pinch the bridge of my nose.

"Of course, we do. C'mon, it'll be fun."

"If you say so…" I grumble and push my chair back, following her to the booth where Burns is already sitting, sniffing my beer.

"What'd you order?"

"The Imperial Stout," Alex tells him.

183

"Is it any good?"

"Yes." I sigh, wondering if I'll ever be able to have a date with Hazel without someone interrupting us.

"I'll take it." Burns puts my beer down and rests his hands on the table.

"I'll have water." Miss Janet smiles at Alex. "I'm driving the old geezer home."

"I'm old but not a geezer," Burn chastises.

"You're both," I grumble.

"Are you two on a date?" Burns asks. "Amber said you missed Sunday dinner because you were with Hazel."

"I just told you they were on a date." Miss Janet frowns at him.

"You did?"

"Yes, you were standing right there when I told you." Miss Janet points to the table we were just sitting at.

"Huh, I didn't hear you." Burns sticks a finger in his ear and wiggles.

"Are you two on a date?" Hazel asks Miss Janet, pressing her lips together when Burns sticks his finger in his other ear.

"Yep. It's our eleven-month wedding anniversary," Burns says loud enough for the entire restaurant to hear.

"Eleven months, congratulations." Hazel nods, wide-eyed, and her lip trembles with held back laughter.

"Burns likes to celebrate big and little things. He was constipated the other day, and we had to a celebration dinner when he was finally able to poo."

"I see." Hazel chokes on her laughter then pretends to cough, and I squeeze her neck and pull her into my side, kissing her temple.

"I'll make this up to you," I whisper.

"I'm having fun," she whispers back.

Burns folds his hands on the table and leans in. "Did Jax ever tell you about the time he went skinny dippin' at the creek near the old barn north of town, and Eric stole his clothes? He walked butt ass naked the entire way home."

"I did hear about that," Hazel says, glancing at me with a blush. I tilt my head and scan her face. I don't think she heard about it but saw it first-hand.

"What about the time he mixed hot sauce in Eric's water bottler during wrestling practice?"

"No, I didn't." Hazel looks up at me, surprised. "Your own brother?"

"He deserved it. I don't think he knows it was me, though." I smile over my beer glass.

"Careful," Miss Janet warns. "You piss Hazel off, she's got leverage over you."

"Hazel's too sweet to do such a thing." I squeeze her side, breathing in her sweet summer scent. At least there is one perk to moving to a booth—closer proximity to Hazel.

"I will *totally* sell you out if you piss me off." Hazel giggles.

"I like her." Burns points at Hazel, smiling like he hit the jackpot.

Alex brings over Burns' beer and Miss Janet's water, taking our order before leaving us to listen to Burns share stories of my brothers and me growing up. Before we know it, our food arrives, but that doesn't stop Burns from rattling off more stories, each becoming more exaggerated and somehow, he's the hero in all of them.

Our ribeyes were mouthwatering and paired great with the Imperial Stout, and I have an idea for a steak pizza to pair with my Stout It Out beer. The garlic mashed potatoes and asparagus were equally delicious. By the time we finish eating, I'm borderline uncomfortably full, especially after Hazel lets me eat her leftovers.

After we pay, I take Hazel's hand, leading her to my truck, feeling a sense of contentment settle over me as we say our goodbyes to Burns and Miss Janet. I may have not liked them butting in on my date, but I do like the way Hazel fits in with my family. I never knew being in a relationship could feel so gratifying and comfortable.

For years I've chased new experiences, itched to go to new places, and find adventure, and then after I found it, I felt the urge to move on. At first it was fun, but after a few years of it, I didn't know what else to do but to keep moving on. Starting *Colson Brewery* broke that cycle, and even though I am doing what I love, I worried I would want to chase after new experiences only to be stuck. Hazel's a new experience, and one I don't think I'll ever tire of. She's becoming my new adventure.

"Did you have fun?" I ask when I climb into the truck and put it into gear.

"I did." She glances over at me, and I take her hand, interlacing our fingers and resting it on my thigh. "Burns and Miss Janet are a hoot."

"They are troublemakers." I squeeze her hand. "And they meddle. And never believe anything Burns says."

"They love you." She sighs, looking out the window at the passing scenery. "Burns really missed you while you were away."

"I will deny ever saying this, but I missed him, too. There are a lot of things I didn't realize I missed until I returned."

"Like what?"

"I didn't realize I missed my brothers until I came back to visit almost a year ago. We were close growing up, but something shifted, and we sort of lost track of each other. After Luke moved back, and Clint and Dawn got married, it was hard to move on, so I just stuck around. Benny selling his bar may have pushed me to open *Colson Brewery*, but I knew before then that I wasn't going to leave again."

"You really are here to stay," she says, her tone filled with relief. I glance over at her, trying to read her face. I don't understand her comment, and I wonder if she still believes I'm not capable of being the kind of man she's looking for.

"I'm here to stay." And I mentally vow to prove to her that I'm the perfect man for her.

"Good," she flexes her fingers around mine, "cause I'm getting used to having you around, too."

11

~ Hazel ~

I might be making a terrible mistake, or I might be making the best decision of my life. Actually, I think I'm doing both. Date number two with Jax was not what I had expected, but it was absolutely perfect... So perfect that I didn't want it to end and invited Jax inside for a drink.

"Are you sure you want me to come in?" Jax asks once my trembling hands manage to unlock my front door.

"I invited you in, didn't I?" I give him a snarky smile, pretending I'm not nervous about having him in my space, looking too good to be true in dress pants and a blue button-down shirt. He trimmed his beard, and his shaggy black hair is combed back. I knew he was capable of dressing up—I saw it at his brother's wedding—but dressing up for me and taking me to a nice restaurant isn't what I had expected. *Jax* isn't what I had expected, and I don't know if I'm scared or excited.

"I'm just checking. You don't always let me know what's going on in that pretty head of yours."

"I do, too." I turn and put my hands on my hips, glaring defiantly at him. "I take pride in being honest with everyone."

"You are definitely honest, but that doesn't mean you share what you're thinking." He comes to stand in front of me, his hands wrapping around my waist. Warm hands that always find a way to touch me and send excited little tingles racing up and down my body. "Like now."

"What do you think I'm not saying?"

"You're nervous."

I so am nervous. I know what I *want* to happen tonight, but I don't know whether I'm ready for that yet. It's been years since I was with a man, and I know Jax isn't lacking in the experience department. We've only been on two dates and my insecurities weigh on me like a heavy coat. I'm not fully sure if Jax is taking this dating thing seriously or if he's just flirting with me until he's ready to move on. I want to believe he is taking it seriously. He's showing me he is, but until I'm certain, I don't think I would be fully comfortable being intimate with him. "Can I get you something to drink?"

"How about we sit down and relax instead?" Jax counters, taking my hand and leading me to the loveseat and pulling me down to sit next to him. His arm wraps around my shoulders, pulling me into his side. I feel the muscles underneath his shirt twitch beneath my hand. I want to spread my hand out and feel more of him, but I bite back the urge. "See, this isn't so bad."

"No, this isn't so bad." I nod, not fully listening to him since I'm too distracted by the hard planes of his chest. I've felt his chest, but I was too distracted by my sorrow to pay attention to how good it felt beneath my hands.

"Do you want to watch something or just sit here and talk?"

Shaking my head, I pull from Jax's side, needing space before I do something embarrassing. I reach for the TV remote. "We can watch something." Flipping on the TV, Jax runs a finger down the center of my back, causing me to shiver. I bite the inside of my cheek to stop the gasp I almost let out. "Wh—" I croak before clearing my throat. "What do you want to watch?"

"Anything that will make you relax." He pulls me back into his side, sliding my hair to the side, giving him access to run a finger down my neck, leaving a fiery trail and causing my brain to short circuit as white-hot desire courses through my body, melting me into his arms. I stop flipping through the channels and clench my thighs, my core overloading with sensations I can't remember feeling before.

"I love when you blush," Jax murmurs close to my ear, his warm breath startling me and I drop the remote. My nerves are shot and only getting worse the more he touches me. I can't say I regret my choice of inviting him in, but I might explode if he continues to caress my skin.

I move to pick up the remote, attempting again to put distance between us when Jax's hands clamp around my waist and he pulls me into his lap. My arms cling to his shoulders at the sudden loss of balance.

"Why are you so nervous," he whispers, tracing his nose down the side of my cheek. Just the lightest of touches from him lights me up. "Hazel, look at me." I peer through my lashes, his playful blue eyes showing a tenderness that eases some of my nerves, and I take a deep breath, drawing in his scent. "What are you thinking?"

"We can't have sex," I blurt out and immediately cover my mouth, looking away as my face heats up. I have to be cherry-red and look away from him. Could this night get any more embarrassing?

"Okay, we don't have to have sex." Jax tugs at my hands, pulling them away from my still-heated face, taking my chin and moving it so his eyes can search mine. "We can go slow."

I don't trust my voice—especially not when I'm staring deep into his eyes, wishing I could read his mind and see how he feels about me. We have a physical connection, there is no denying that, but could we have an emotional connection?

"Can I kiss you?" he whispers, and I lick my lips. His eyes zero in on my mouth, his pupils dilating.

"Yes—"

His mouth covers my own, cutting off my words as his tongue tangles with mine. The fiery heat his touch made is nothing compared to the volcanic inferno his tongue is doing to me. My nipples stiffen and my body moves on its own volition, straddling his lap and feeling him harden beneath me.

This is not going slow. My self-control is gone, lost when his mouth touched mine and showed me what his tongue is capable of. His kisses grow more demanding as he fists my hair and pulls me tight against his chest.

The front door crashes open, banging loudly and echoes through my house, breaking Jax and me apart. "Fucking hell, Haz—" Warren stares shocked into the house before snapping his mouth shut. His shocked stare shifts into a glare, his mouth pinches together, and he fists his hands.

"What the hell, McKnight," Jax yells over his shoulder that's pinned beneath me. I make to move from his lap, but he holds me tight. "Don't you knock?"

"Get up," Warren yells, charging into my house. "Get up! Now!"

I scramble off Jax's lap, tugging my dress down. Jax moves me behind him, blocking me from Warren, who comes to stand toe to toe with Jax. "Time to leave, Jax."

"I don't think that's your call," Jax growls as he sizes my brother up.

"Hazel, tell Jax goodbye," Warren orders, not taking his eyes off Jax.

"No." I jerk my head back. "Why are you here and barging through my door?" Warren shifts his glare from Jax to me, and I raise a brow at him, crossing my arms over my chest and tapping my foot. "Well?"

"One of my deputies saw a truck they didn't recognize in your driveway," he answers, taking the smallest step away from Jax.

"You know what my truck looks like," Jax hisses.

Warren doesn't say anything but looks over at the open front door. "Why didn't you make sure to lock her door?" He throws an accusing finger at Jax's chest. "I told you to be cautious."

Jax presses his lips together, glancing over his shoulder at me with concern. "You're right. I should have locked the door behind me, but that doesn't give you the right to barge in."

"Hazel's my sister. I always have the right to barge in."

"Being my brother doesn't give you that right at all." I slap my hands on my hips. Warren has never been over-the-top protective of me before; there is something he isn't saying. I can see it in the weary look he gives me. "What's going on, Warren?"

"I told you to be cautious. We have a murderer wandering the streets, and we aren't any closer to catching him than we were the other day."

"I appreciate your concern for my well-being, but I have been cautious."

"Leaving your door unlocked is *not* being cautious, Hazel."

"Is Hazel in danger?" Jax demands, cutting into our bickering. The hairs on the back of my neck raise and I look at Warren for answers. Am I in danger and he isn't telling me for my own protection? I'd like to believe my brother would be forthcoming about something as serious as being a potential target, but his behavior and the secretive warnings lead me to believe otherwise.

Warren runs a hand down his face. "Everyone is in danger while that murderer is free."

Jax's brow pulls down into a deep V. His arm snakes around my waist and pulls me into his side, concern in his eyes, before shifting his attention back to Warren. "I'll make sure the house is locked up tight before I go."

Warren narrows his eyes at Jax. "I'll do that."

"No, you won't." I shake my head. "You've invaded my personal space enough."

Warren looks taken aback and opens his mouth to say something but decides against it. Without a word, he turns his back on us and walks out the front door, slamming it shut behind him.

"He's going to sit outside your house until I leave, isn't he?" Jax thumbs at the front door.

"Yep." I sigh, leaning into Jax's side, wrapping an arm around his waist, and letting his warmth wash away the chill my brother let in. Jax pulls me into his chest and kisses the top of my head. "I'm sorry." I tilt my head up and rest my chin on his chest.

"For what?" He tucks a strand of hair behind my ear.

"For my brother barging in and ruining everything."

"We're even now," Jax says with a heart-melting smiling. His head drops, placing a warm kiss against my lips, but he doesn't let it go further than that. "I should go."

"Yeah," I agree, disappointment squeezing my heart. I want to do more of that kissing we were doing earlier, but he's right. He should leave before my brother comes back and tries to force him out or worse, I lose my self-control again.

"I'll come over tomorrow after work," Jax says, releasing me. "We can relax and watch TV."

"That sounds great." I smile, hoping tomorrow I won't lose my self-control and we really do take things slow.

*****

"Hello," a familiar voice calls as the bells chime from over the front door of my office. "Hazel, you here?"

"I'm here." I walk through the conference room door into the lobby to greet Amber and Dawn. I called Amber yesterday after I finished retouching her wedding photos; we talked on the phone for almost an hour before scheduling a time to meet today. Her genuine interest in my life touched me, and I've been excited to see her and Dawn ever since. "Hi, ladies."

"This place looks amazing," Dawn says, looking around the small lobby at the photos on display. I worked hard to make this place aesthetically pleasing, catching the eye of people who pass by. It seems to be working as I've had a lot of foot traffic. My schedule is booking up quickly, and I may be able to hire someone to man the lobby desk.

"I especially like the large canvas photo of Luke and me. If the rest of the photos look as good as that one, I underpaid you for the wedding." Amber smiles with excitement.

"Do you ladies want some coffee before we get started?" I point over to the break area where I put together a charcuterie board of snacks and a small plater of cookies.

"I never turn down coffee." Amber laughs. "Sarah wanted to be here, but she's too pregnant to go anywhere. I told her I would say hi."

Caught off-guard, I blink before quickly recovering and sending my regards to Sarah. I haven't spoken to any of them since our Sunday dinner two weeks ago, but then again, I've been busy with photoshoots or working on Jax's branding by day and kissing him by night. He has come over every night and we spend the evening together. He promised to take things slow and that is exactly what he's been doing, not letting our make-out sessions go too far, even if it is driving me crazy. He's even skipped his family Sunday dinners to have dinner with my mom and me. Warren wasn't happy to hear about Jax coming and made excuses for not coming. He hasn't showed up at my house unannounced, either. I'm going to have to confront him soon.

"You didn't have to do this for us," Amber says, reminding me that I have guests. No, not guests… *friends*.

"Of course, I had to pull out the red carpet for you. You were my first client and thanks to you, I've booked three more appointments to do family photos."

"Don't let me forget, I need to schedule an appointment before we leave," Dawn says, dropping a tea bag into some hot water. "I hope you aren't too busy with Jax's stuff and other appointments to squeeze me in soon."

"She's going to want to get pictures before she starts showing," Amber chimes in, stirring creamer into her coffee. Then she looks up at

Dawn with a guilty look. "I'm so sorry… I didn't mean to spill the beans."

Dawn laughs and playfully elbows Amber. "It's fine."

"You're pregnant?" I ask, a smile widening across my face. I've never taken pregnancy photos before, but ideas are already running through my head.

"Yes, but not everyone knows yet. I'll tell everyone at Sunday dinner. Do you think you and Jax could come to dinner on Sunday?"

"This Sunday?"

"Yes, this Sunday."

"I usually have Sunday dinner with my mom." I frown.

"Your mom is welcome to come, unless you think all of us will be too much for her," Amber adds. I forgot she knew about my mother's Alzheimer's. "How's she doing, by the way?"

"As good as can be. She doesn't seem to remember what happened, and I guess that's good, but it gave me a scare," I admit. "I'll talk to her about coming to dinner, but I'll make sure Jax goes, and your secret is safe with me."

"I'm glad your mom is okay. If you ever need any help, you've got my number." Dawn squeezes my hand and I'm struck with the genuine friendship these ladies are extending to me. "Oh, and Warren is welcome to come, too."

"I don't think that's a good idea. Warren is barely talking to me."

"Why?" Amber asks, popping a grape into her mouth.

"He's mad…" I trail off, not wanting them to be upset but not sure how to explain it without doing so.

"Because you're dating Jax," Amber finishes for me. "Of course, he would be. Until recently, the McKnight clan, present company excluded, has hated the Colsons. Although, you would think him and Eric being friends again would have changed things."

"He and Clint get along," Dawn points out.

"I'm not a McKnight," I pipe up. "Warren Sr. isn't my dad."

"He's not?" Amber looks surprised.

"No, my mom remarried."

"I bet you're happy not to have Warren Sr. as a dad," Dawn adds. "The man scares me, and I know scary."

"I'm blessedly happy he isn't my dad, and he scares me, too." I laugh, relieved my brother isn't ruining my chance at friendship.

"We need to hang out more." Amber points her coffee spoon at me. "You should come to our semi-regular, but not at all consistent, girls get-together."

"I'd love to." I giggle at her description. "I'll bring the wine… or wait, with two of you pregnant, does that mean girl get-togethers are alcohol-free?"

"Absolutely not." Amber shakes her head. "It only means we have designated drivers."

"Sarah's going to be upset if we go without her." Dawn taps her chin. "We'll have to go over to her house."

"When are you free?" Amber asks, pulling her phone out. "I've got this weekend off, but Matt has a basketball game at ten."

"I'm free Saturday. Any day really."

"Great, I'll tell Sarah we're coming over Saturday afternoon." Amber taps on her phone. "Jax won't mind us taking up all your time?"

"Oh no, he won't mind. It's not like we're serious or anything… just dating." The words give me a sour taste in my mouth, and Dawn and Amber share a look.

"I think you two are more than just dating." Dawn gives me a sympathetic smile.

"You do?"

"I mean, Jax hasn't come out and said it, but I've never seen him like this over a girl before," Amber adds.

I'm not sure what to say to that and if I don't change the subject, I'll likely share with them I'm hopeful that Jax will tell me soon that he wants to be in a serious relationship. However, after spending every available moment with him these last two weeks, he hasn't indicated he wanted anything more. If anything, he makes sure we take things slow and while a small piece of me appreciates that, a larger piece of me fears he's holding back because he isn't sure it's what he wants. "Are you ready to look at the photos?"

"Yes please," Amber says, and I lead them into the small conference room where I have my laptop hooked up to a TV.

We look through hundreds of photos for the next hour while talking about everything and nothing. We laugh until our sides hurt when we spot Burns and Miss Janet making out in the background of one of the photos I hadn't retouched. We laugh harder when we get to the pictures of Burns and Miss Janet dancing, and I learned they have a tendency to dance provocatively in public. By the time we are done, I'm sad to see them go. We were having so much fun, but Dawn has to get back to work at Clint's autobody shop and Amber has to pick up her kids from school.

"You better come this Saturday. You can't bail. You're one of us now," Amber warns, opening the front door and the bells chime.

"We know how to find you," Dawn adds, walking through the open door. "And we aren't afraid to come get you."

"You two are trouble." I laugh, excited for Saturday and spending more time with Jax's family. "I promise I'll come." We wave goodbye and I shut the door, unable to pretend I haven't completely fallen for Jax, but what's worse... I've completely fallen for his family.

Picture Forever

12

~ Jax ~

I've screwed up. I don't know how I screwed up, but I know I did something to cause Hazel to distance herself from me. First, she wanted to head to bed early, cutting our evening together short, and then the next day, I barely got any time with her because she wanted to spend the evening with her mom. Today she's heading over to Sarah's house for girl time and wasn't sure when it would end. She also told me I couldn't come to Sunday dinner because I was expected to be at Amber and Luke's.

I may be new at being a boyfriend, but I know when I'm being blown off, and she is blowing me off… again. I don't care if I have to wait all damn night, I'm going to get to the bottom of this tonight.

"Jax, you here?" Eric's voice calls from the front of *Colson Brewery*. Too wound up to sit around my apartment, I came in to get a batch of Spicy Bumpkin started. The Fall Festival is just around the corner, and Hazel's almost finished with my branding. If everything falls into place, I can set up a booth at the Fall Festival and introduce *Colson Brewery* to Peak Valley and start spreading the word of the grand opening in late October.

"I'm back here," I yell at Eric, not surprised he'd dip out when all the women showed up at his house for girl time. What the hell is girl time, anyway? Is it code for something? I'll have to ask Eric.

Eric comes through the door leading into the back area where I'm working, and he isn't alone. McKnight stands behind Eric, looking determined, and my stomach drops, wondering if his appearance has anything to do with Hazel distancing herself.

"Do you mind coming out front to have a few words with McKnight?" Eric scratches the back of his neck and I straighten.

"What's this about?"

"McKnight wants to have chat. Man to man. Right?" Eric glances over his shoulder at McKnight.

"Right," McKnight says through a clenched jaw.

"Fine." I pull the rubber gloves off my hands and throw them onto my worktable before following Eric and McKnight out of the work area and into the customer seating area. Luke brought over a couple of tables and chairs I custom ordered from him, and Eric turns a chair around, straddling the seat, and resting his arms over the top, looking mildly entertained. Me, I'm feeling mildly annoyed.

McKnight paces aggressively across the floor, his footsteps thud while fisting his hands open and closed.

"Start talking, I've got shit to do." I cross my arms over my chest, earning me a glare from McKnight.

McKnight stops and mirrors my stance. "I've seen your truck at Hazel's house every night for the last two weeks. I know you're going to my mom's house for dinner, but what I can't figure out is why."

"Isn't it obvious?" I jerk my head back and hold my arms out wide. "We're together."

"Could you be serious for once in your life?" McKnight runs a frustrated hand through his hair. His agitation is wearing on my already frayed nerves.

"I am *serious*," I growl, then look at Eric. "Why are you here?"

"McKnight thought I could help knock some sense into you."

"You're taking his side?" I point at McKnight. I know Eric and McKnight just became friends, they even work together on occasion, but I never expected Eric to take his side over mine.

"I'm not taking sides," Eric holds his hands up. "I'm here to play mediator."

"This is fucking ridiculous." I roll my shoulders. "Let me say this slowly for you. I'm with Hazel, and I will continue to be with Hazel until *she* tells me it's over. You can either accept that or you can get lost."

"I don't trust you." McKnight glares at me. "Hazel isn't the kind of woman you have a fling with."

"You don't have to trust me, she does, and she isn't a *fling*." I want to throttle the man and would if he wasn't the fucking sheriff. "And I don't have to justify myself to you."

"Eric, you know Jax. Do you really think he's not just stringing my sister along?" McKnight looks to Eric for help.

Eric studies me for a moment, his face unreadable before he turns to McKnight. "He isn't stringing your sister along."

McKnight swears under his breath and turns his back, and I think he's about to storm out when he turns on his heels and points his finger at me. "I meant what I said, I will tear this place to the ground if you so much as make her cry."

I'd gladly let him tear this place to the ground if I ever make Hazel cry. I've held her while she cried, and it gutted me. "You have my permission to tear this place brick by brick if it ever happens."

McKnight's pointed finger falls to his side, surprise written across his face. He looks from me to Eric, then back at me. I don't think I've ever seen the man speechless, but I meant every word I said. I care about Hazel, more than I've ever cared for a woman. I like being in a relationship and I don't want it to end, and I'll do my best to fix whatever the hell is going on where she thinks she needs to put distance between us.

Eric's phone goes off, breaking the silence. "If we're done here, can I get back to work?" I ask while Eric puts his phone to his ear and nods at me.

I glance at McKnight, who can't seem to figure out if he wants to kick my ass or bury my body when Eric stands abruptly, knocking over the chair he's straddling. It bangs against the floor, and both McKnight and I crowd around him.

"I'm on my way," he says, a stunned look on his face while I pick up the chair and wait for an explanation.

"What's going on?" McKnight asks, the impatient bastard.

"It's Sarah. She's in labor."

McKnight and I share a look before I grab Eric's shoulder. "You gotta go. We all gotta go." Then I point at McKnight. "Can you escort us?"

"The hospital is five blocks away, you don't need a fucking escort." McKnight rolls his eyes, then waves for us to move. "Go."

"I'll drive." I push Eric toward the door. "Are you excited? You're about to be a father."

"I'm about to be a father." He nods and follows me as we make a beeline out the door and to my truck.

*****

"Are you sure I should be here?" Hazel whispers to me for the tenth time.

"Yes, you should be here." I wrap a hand around her neck and squeeze it gently, pulling her close and kissing her temple. It's been four hours since I drove Eric to the hospital, and he slipped behind the doors leading to Sarah's waiting room. He's come out a few times to give us updates, but that was over an hour ago and everyone is getting anxious. "I'm glad you're here with me."

Hazel peers up at me, her brown eyes full of questions, and I'm about to ask her about it when Eric comes through the doors with the biggest fucking smile on his face. We all stand, waiting for him to speak.

"Sarah and Ericah are doing fine," Eric shares. "She's perfect, and Sarah was amazing."

"Can we see her?" Linda, Sarah's mom, asks. Luke and Amber are standing behind her. Dawn and Clint just went to feed Axel in a quiet place but will be back soon, and Burns and Miss Janet remain seated next to Hazel and me.

"As soon as they finish cleaning her up and running their tests, you all are welcome to come in and meet Ericah. I know you all are excited to see her, but Sarah is tired. Can we keep the visit short so she can get some rest, and I promise as soon as I have them both home safe and sound, you can come over for another visit."

"How big was she?" Burns asks, and everyone groans. When Clint and Dawn had Axel, Burns set a bet on how big the boy would be. Burns, not having much experience with babies, thought the baby was going to be over twenty pounds. I'm surprised he didn't try for another bet this time around.

"Nine pounds, and she's twenty-one inches. She has all her fingers and toes and looks just like Sarah," Eric says full of pride and for a moment, I envy him. I never once thought about having children. I love children, but it never was something I felt compelled to ponder. Looking down at Hazel, I don't need to ask if she wants children—my gut tells me she does. She wants the house and the two-point-five children with a long-lasting marriage, and none of that scares me.

We wait another hour before we're allowed to go back into Sarah's hospital room. Hazel and I stand in the back, letting Sarah's parents get in to see Ericah and Sarah before they let Amber and Luke hold her. Hazel grows more anxious the longer we wait our turn.

"You okay?" I whisper, pulling her into my side so the others can't hear us. "You seem nervous."

"I'm a little nervous."

"Why?"

She licks her lips and nibbles on her thumb nail. "I've never held a baby before."

"You haven't?" I tilt my head and scan her face.

"A few ladies I worked with had babies, but they never brought them into the office, and I wasn't close enough friends with them that I thought I should visit them at the hospital."

"I've seen you with my niece and nephews, you'll do fine."

"You think so?"

I laugh and squeeze her waist. "It isn't hard. I've held Axel. If I can do it, you can do it."

"Yeah, you're right." She nods, still nibbling her thumb.

"C'mon, let's get our turn before Burns cuts in." I take Hazel's hand and lead her to Sarah's bedside, where her and Amber are chatting, Ericah in Amber's arms.

"Hazel, I'm glad you stayed," Sarah says with a tired smile. "I'm sorry I ruined girl time."

"You didn't ruin anything." Hazel laughs and leans in close to Amber, peering down at Ericah. "She's precious."

"Do you want to hold her?" Amber asks.

"Yes, she would," I answer for her. "She's never held a baby before."

"You haven't?" Amber asks, adjusting Ericah in her arms to hand to Hazel.

"Is that okay?" Hazel looks at Sarah for confirmation.

"It's fine. I'm happy Ericah gets to be your first baby." Sarah waves.

Hazel holds her arms out and listens intently to Amber's instructions before stiffly taking Ericah into her arms. Ericah doesn't make a peep and settles into Hazel's arms, sound asleep, relaxing Hazel and coaxing out a sweet smile. She doesn't take her eyes off Ericah, and I don't take my eyes off Hazel holding my niece. The more I experience being in a relationship, the more I wonder why I never gave it a try, but I know why. None of the women I was ever with can hold a candle to Hazel. She's the kind of woman you spend forever with, and spending forever with her just might be my next great adventure.

Picture Forever

13

~ Hazel ~

I have baby fever. I always wanted to have kids, expected I would have them someday, but was never in a hurry to find Mr. Right and start making them. Ericah changed that the moment I held her in my arms. I never held something so precious before; she truly is a bundle of joy and she turned my biological clock on, and I don't know if there is a snooze button.

"You ready to leave?" Jax whispers in my ear. I've been staring down at Ericah as everyone wished the happy couple congratulations before leaving. I just didn't realize we were the only ones left.

"No, I want to hold her again." I run a finger along her cheek.

"I'm sure Eric and Sarah will be happy to know you'll babysit for them whenever they want." Jax takes my hand and squeezes it. "But we should go, Sarah looks beat."

I turn around and wave at Eric and Sarah, who both look exhausted but happy. "Congratulations, you two. I'm so happy for you both."

"Thank you, Hazel." Sarah waves. "I'll have you and Jax over soon."

As we leave and our steps on the linoleum echo against the white walls, my thoughts turn toward Jax and us. I don't want things to end between us, but I also don't want to slip into complacency. He and his family are becoming important to me, becoming special and merging into my life. I like spending time with him, hearing about his adventures, or just watching TV, but I want this relationship to go somewhere before I invest my whole self, only to be destroyed when he isn't willing or ready to do the same.

Sirens from an approaching ambulance pierce the air when the automatic doors open for us as we exit. We make it two feet out before Jax tugs on my hand, and I stop and look up at him. He's looking across the parking lot where Warren is heading toward us. Jax doesn't say anything, but he waits for Warren to walk to us, his jaw clenched and tension rolling off Jax's shoulders. He and Warren have been at each other's throats since the beginning. Warren fears the same thing I fear, and I'm being a little hypocritical when I call Warren out for it, but he isn't living my life. I am and I need to be the one to make decisions, even if they lead me to heart ache.

"Warren, I think it's too late for you to see Eric and Sarah. Sarah was about to fall asleep when we left," I say when he gets close.

"I'm not here to see them. I'm here on police business." Warren reaches for me, pulling me into his arms, and giving me a tight squeeze.

"Is Mom okay?" I mumble, smothered into his chest and praying he isn't here to deliver bad news. "Did something happen?"

"Mom is fine. I have a patrol car parked at her house." Warren releases me from his bear hug only to extend his hand to Jax. I do a double take and my mouth falls open before I snap it shut. Jax hesitates before shaking his hand as the animosity between them disappears.

"What just happened here?" I point between them.

Warren ignores me and turns to face Jax. "I need you to go home with Hazel and stay there."

Jax's brow furrows. "What's going on?"

"There was an assault on Judge Rightfield's son. He just arrived in critical condition," Warren shares, glancing at the ambulance bay. "Everyone needs to be on high alert."

"Do you think the person who assaulted Rightfield's son is the same guy who murdered Kevin Hunt's wife?"

"I don't know. A paramedic said the boy was mumbling, 'she said an eye for an eye.'"

"He was attacked by a woman?" I gasp, covering my mouth. How could a woman attack a child? "How old is the boy?"

"Twelve. He put up a good fight, he managed to fight his way free. A neighbor heard him screaming and came outside to see what was going on. They saw the boy laying in the lawn and a small figure wearing a black hoodie running off."

"That's terrible," I whisper, Jax pulling me into his side.

"Do you think she's targeting people who work in the justice system? Have you warned Eric?"

"I'm about to." Warren nods. "I need to get inside. You two be careful." Warren points at Jax. "I mean it, don't leave her alone."

"I won't." Jax nods and takes my hand. "I'm taking her back to my place."

"Good idea." Warren sidesteps us. "Let's talk about an alarm system at Hazel's later."

"Call me when you're free, and I'll set it up. Eric isn't going to have time now that he has a newborn," Jax says, and I wonder if they realize I'm standing right here. Shouldn't they be asking me if they can install an alarm system? I'm not against it, and after the bombshell Warren just dropped, I'd feel better having one, but I still want a say in it.

"I'll call you tomorrow." Warren waves and Jax leads me out toward the parking lot.

"Hand me your keys." Jax holds out a hand.

"Why?"

"So I can drive us to my place."

"You aren't taking your truck?" I scan the parking lot.

"I'm leaving it for Eric to drive. He'll drop it off after he gets Sarah and Ericah home."

"Oh." I pull my keys from my purse. "I need to pick up a few things."

"It'll have to wait." Jax takes the keys and the car beeps, unlocking the doors. "It's late and I want to get you somewhere safe."

"Jax, I don't have anything to wear… I'll be quick."

"You can wear one of my shirts." Jax opens my door and winks, waving me to get in.

We're on the road heading for Jax's apartment, and the closer we get, the more nervous I feel.

"You and Warren seem to be getting along," I say, the silence making me more anxious.

"We talked."

"When?" I shift around to see him, surprised Warren would even give Jax the time of day.

"Earlier today," Jax grunts.

"What did you guys talk about?"

"That's between me and him." Jax glances at me with a flirty smile. "We are good. Are you hungry?"

"Not really? Amber, Dawn, and I raided the vending machine earlier," I say, staring outside my window. I'm too nervous to eat, anyway. I've never been to his apartment before. Jax has been coming to my house, claiming he'd rather be the one who drives home late at night. It's another thing he does that makes it hard not to fall for him and take it slow until he figures out what he wants. Or should I confront him and ask him where he sees this relationship between us going?

Being at Jax's house, wearing his shirt, sleeping in his bed, I don't think I'm going to be able to keep my self-control in tack. I don't want to hold back, I want to move forward… I just don't know how to nudge us over that hump, and a part of me is scared to find out what Jax wants. Dating has been amazing, and I love spending time with him. It's hard not to progress naturally to the next step, but Jax's inexperience in the relationship department makes me second-guess everything.

Jax pulls my car into a narrow parking spot to the side of *Clint's Autobody,* where a staircase leads to Jax's apartment. I climb out of the car and Jax is by my side before I can shut the door and we climb the steps. My stomach turns into a tighter knot with each step.

When he opens the apartment door, I didn't expect to see a modern-styled apartment. I pictured wood-paneled walls, yellowing kitchenette, and a futon; but instead, he has a spacious apartment with a cozy couch and a recliner facing a massive TV. The kitchen is separated by a huge island with stools lining it. Black granite countertops shine beneath track lighting and his stainless-steel appliances are the size you would see in a master chef's kitchen, not a bachelor pad.

"This is not what I expected," I say, walking deeper into the apartment while Jax turns on the security alarm. Laying my purse on the kitchen island, I do a slow turn, taking the whole place in. It's amazing, but it lacks décor and personal touches. He doesn't have any pictures of his family or art, not even a book on display. So many ideas and possibilities pop into my head.

"Clint remodeled it several years ago before he met Dawn. He never thought he would meet someone, so he made himself comfortable."

I wander over to a sliding glass door and peer out into the night. "You have a balcony?"

"Yeah, but the view isn't great. Just looks over Clint's junkyard."

"Can I see?"

"Be my guest." Jax follows me out onto the balcony, sliding it shut behind him. He shoves his hands into his pockets, letting me scan over the piles of scrap metal and rows of cars. He's right, it isn't much of a view, but there is something peaceful to it. I could see Clint liking the view.

Fall has officially taken over, and with it, chilly nights. I let out a shiver that catches Jax's attention and he takes my hand. "Let's get you inside." And with that, he leads me back into his apartment.

We have spent a lot of time together for several weeks now, but being in his apartment, alone with him, feels more intimate.

Jax's hands curve around my waist, his touch like a match igniting gasoline and setting my whole body ablaze. "I've missed seeing you," he murmurs close to my ear.

"You have?" I peer up into his blue eyes, wishing they were windows into his soul. It isn't that I don't believe him, it's that I *do*. I believe everything he says, everything he does, yet his past makes it hard for me to trust him. I've come to believe he's genuine in his actions, even his words.

His entire family is genuine, but being genuine and knowing what you want are two different things. I don't trust he knows what he wants, which puts me in a precarious spot. I'm clinging to a cliff's edge, faced with two options, let go and fall or be worn down and fall. Either way, I'm in too deep with Jax.

"I like seeing you." He nods, his fingers tracing up my spine, fueling the already fiery arousal coursing through me. "I don't like the distance you've been putting between us."

"I wasn't putting distance between us." I shake my head with a frown. I was taking a step back. Trying to slow my trajectory.

"Then what do you call it?"

"Giving us a little space, to breathe and make sure this is what we want."

"Are you having doubts?"

"Are you?"

"None," Jax whispers with the gorgeous smile of his. He pulls me into his chest and his incredible scent tickles my nose as his arms band around me, making my choice to let go much more enticing.

His lips seek out mine, releasing a floodgate of desire that makes my knees weak and I cling to him. Pressing my chest against him, my nipples harden and when his hand fists my hair, I let out a gasp. Jax breaks off the kiss, resting his forehead against mine, and I can feel him harden against my lower belly. "We need to slow it down."

I exhale all the air in my lungs, unsatisfied. "I don't want to slow it down."

Jax's pulls his head back, his eyes searching my face, looking for a trace of doubt. There is a little doubt, but I'm letting go and moving forward. "Are you sure?"

"I'm tired of going slow. I don't want to go slow, not anymore. I like you, Jax, really like you, and I don't want to be in this holding pattern. Not anymore."

Jax doesn't comment, he doesn't say a word but picks me up, his arms like a steel vice around me, and carries me down a hallway off the kitchen into a dark room. It must be his bedroom as the back of my knees hit something soft before I'm falling onto a cloud of softness, Jax laying over me and his beard tickling my neck with hot, desperate kisses.

His body spreads open my thighs and even through our clothes, I can feel just how hard he is. My legs wrap around his waist and my hands tug on his shirt while he continues to blaze a trail up my neck. "Do you know how many times I've jacked off dreaming of this moment?" he whispers in my ear, his hand moving under my shirt and tracing the side of my breast to the top of my bra, following the edge causing wetness to soak my panties.

"Take my clothes off," I pant, forgetting all my inhibitions as I yank on his shirt. Pushing up on his knees, his hand goes to the back of his neck and pulls off his shirt, his impressive chest ripped with toned muscles making my mouth dry.

"Now your turn." He tugs on my shirt, and I sit up, making it easier for him. Frantically, we tear at each other's clothes, kicking off our shoes and tossing them into the darkness of the room.

Lying back, both of us undressed, Jax opens his bedside table drawer. I hear the tear of the condom more than I see it, then his hands roam up my calf, over my knee, kissing my stomach then my breast, his tongue swirling around my harden nipple and I arch my back on a gasp. Running my hands through his hair, he runs his tongue along my collarbone, settling himself between my legs, nudging my entrance.

"Are you sure you want this?" His voice is tight with restraint.

"Yes," I moan, lifting my hips and helping him slide in with one smooth thrust. I cry out with both pleasure and pain because it's been so long, yet he fits perfectly inside me.

"*Fuck*," Jax growls through clenched teeth, his mouth pressing hard against mine before ripping it away, his head falling back and swearing through his teeth.

My legs wrap around his waist, sinking him in deeper, anxious to start moving. My orgasm is already starting to build, and he swears again before his hips begin to thrust into me, slow and steady. I don't want slow and steady; I want him to let go just like I have. I'm no longer dangling off a cliff but free falling.

"Jax…"

"Fuck, you feel good," he growls at the same time. "Is this okay?"

"No." My thighs squeeze his waist, and he stops his slow pace, and I mewl, trying to get us moving again. "I want to go faster, don't stop."

Jax pulls almost all the way out of me before thrusting in, his pace picking up and my nails digging into his skin. Each thrust fills me with pleasure I have never experienced before. In and out, his thrust fuels my orgasm until I come hard, harder than I ever have before, sending orgasmic shockwaves from my core through my body. Jax pumps harder, drawing out my orgasm until he lets out a swear, releasing himself inside me, and collapsing on top of me.

He rolls to his side, bringing me with him and tucking me into his chest, our legs tangled as we fight to calm our breathing. We stay wrapped in each other's embrace until I drift off to sleep.

14

~ Jax ~

Hazel lets out sharp cry, her finger fisting my hair and her thighs trembling while I drive my tongue deep inside her, her delicious juices coating my mouth as she comes hard. I knew she would taste incredible.

Before her orgasm fades, I slip on another condom and root myself deep inside her. I can't get enough of her. One taste wasn't enough. I woke her up two more times, her scent waking me from blissful dreams, only I didn't have to beat off to them in the shower. I had her beside me in my bed.

Waking up before her, I dove under the covers, needing to taste her before I made us breakfast.

A whimper escapes her lips as I pick up the pace, thrusting in and out of her tight folds. Nothing has ever felt so good. She raises her hips in time with me and her eyes squeeze shut. "Open your eyes," I grunt.

Her brown eyes are almost black with lust and my dick swells. She has been and will continue to be my undoing. My thrusts grow more powerful as the pressure building becomes so intense, I come hard, releasing deep inside her.

My forehead falls to her chest and her hands curl around the back of my neck, tangling in my hair as she releases a sigh that makes my heart soar.

"Are you hungry?" I kiss between her breasts, spent but still inside her. I don't want to break our connection, not after she let go of whatever was holding her back and let me in.

Her stomach growls, and I push up to grin down at her. "I could eat."

"I only have cereal." I frown at her. "Unless you want to run to Clint and Dawn's for breakfast."

"Is that what you normally do?"

"Of course. Have you had Dawn's breakfast burritos?"

"Cereal is fine." She laughs, pushing up and planting a kiss against my lips.

"On second thought, let's take a shower together."

Hazel joins me in the shower, her sun-kissed skin turning pink from the hot water or from the orgasm my fingers gave her—either way, the colors her skin turns drives me wild.

"What do you have planned for today?" I ask with a mouthful of cereal.

"I want to check on my mom." Hazel bites her lip. It's the first time since she came over that she looks nervous.

"Are you worried about her?"

"Not worried… more like I need peace of mind that she's okay. Warren seems overly protective, and I understand why, but there is something he isn't saying."

"Like what?"

"Like why he thinks they would come after me or our mom."

"Does he need a reason?"

"No, I guess not…"

"Mind if I tag along to visit your mom?"

"Sure." She shrugs and dips her spoon into her Cap'n Crunch cereal.

"Do you want to stay here tonight or your place?"

Surprised, Hazel looks up, her cheeks turning pink. "Which would you prefer?"

"I'd like you to stay here until we get a security system installed at your place."

"Okay, we can stay here. I'll pack a bag when you take me back to my place."

"Make sure you pack for several nights." I shovel a spoonful of cereal into my mouth.

Hazel's bright smile spreads across her face. *Damn,* I love that smile.

*****

"Why are we going to Jax's family dinner?" Maria asks again, and I look to Hazel for answers. She's being very tight-lipped about our presence being required at dinner tonight.

"Just trust me, Mom, we need to be there," Hazel groans, letting her head fall against the back of her seat as I drive the ladies to Amber and Luke's house.

"Eric and Sarah aren't even going to be there," I point out.

"I know, but they don't need to be there."

"But we do?" Maria asks, and I nod my head in agreement.

"Well, no… but Jax needs to be there."

"You know something I don't?" I arch a brow at her.

"I'm shutting my mouth. I don't want to give anything away."

Maria taps Hazel's shoulder from the back seat. "Is Warren coming?"

"He said he would try to swing by."

"Does Warren know?"

"I plead the fifth."

"If Warren knows before I do, I will tickle you so my family can hear you cackle like a hyena."

"I don't cackle like a hyena."

"You do, dear, and you also screech like a barn owl."

"You two," Hazel shifts in her seat pointing a finger between Maria and me, "are not allowed to team up on me. You either take my side or no side."

"That isn't how it works, Hazel. I take whoever's side is right." Maria shakes her head and wags a finger.

"And I happen to be right this time." I pull behind Luke's truck and flash Hazel a flirty smile and wiggle my brows at her.

"I don't find you amusing," she grumbles and climbs out of her car. I open Maria's door and help her get out, glad that we took Hazel's car, even though Eric dropped my truck off. Maria's spry for her age, but climbing in and out of the truck would be too taxing on her. I'm going to need to remember that in the future.

Burns is standing on the front porch waiting for us as we approach. "Janet, the jackwagon showed up, and he brought guests."

"See, Burns, I told you he would be here." Miss Janet joins Burns right as we get to the stairs. "Maria, I'm so glad you came."

"Janet? I didn't know you'd be here. What a pleasant surprise." Maria and Miss Janet embrace before Miss Janet leads her into the house.

"Burns, it's always such a *treat* to see you." I smirk at him.

"I'm sorry, Burns. I know I've kept Jax away from his family," Hazel apologizes and squeezes Burns' hand.

"You haven't kept me from anything." I tuck her into my side and kiss her temple.

"Got any idea what's going on? Miss Janet said I had to be here… not like I wasn't going to come."

"She knows," I point at Hazel, "but she won't say."

"All you women keeping secrets is dangerous. Don't you know we do stupid shit trying to find them out?" Burns tugs on a suspender.

"No, I didn't know that, but I'll be sure to remember that in the future." Hazel giggles.

"Hazel, get your butt in here," Amber calls from somewhere in the house.

"Coming." She pulls away from my side and enters the house.

"I don't like this." Burns watches Hazel as she hugs Amber, then Dawn in the kitchen, all three of them wearing excited smiles.

"You don't like being excluded. I'm sure they plan to share whatever it is they're keeping a secret."

"Uncle Jax!" Emily screeches, running full speed toward me. Opening my arms, I scoop her up and give her a big bear hug.

"How's my little human today?" I tap her nose.

"I'm good." She squirms in my arms as I carry her into the house. "Mom said you went on a date with Hazel. Can I come on the next one?"

"Of course, you can," Burns butts in, messing up her hair and taking a seat on the living room couch.

"Yay!" Emily pumps her arms. "Can Parker come, too?"

"Who's Parker."

"He was my boyfriend, but Luke said I had to break up with him because I'm not old enough to date. But now that I'm going on a date with you, he can be my boyfriend again."

"What the hell is going on?" Luke demands as I enter the house, still holding a squirming Emily and shut the door.

"Parker and I are going on a date with Uncle Jax and Aunt Hazel."

Aunt Hazel?

I like the sound of that. Looking over at Hazel, her cheeks turn pink and her eyes widen.

"*Damn it, Emily*! I told you, you aren't allowed to date, and I don't like Parker." Luke groans, then points at me. "Stop encouraging her."

Putting Emily down, I hold my hands up. "I'm not encouraging anything."

"Mom said if Uncle Jax and Aunt Hazel say it's okay to go on a date with them, I could." Emily slaps her little hands on her hips and cocks it out with a challenging grin on her face. "That means I can date."

"That doesn't mean you can date. You're not allowed to date, *ever*. You're going to live with us forever." Luke narrows his eyes, then flashes his own challenging grin. "I will eat any boy you try to date."

"Will not! You're a good giant."

"Not when it comes to boys trying to date my daughter," Luke fires back, and Emily's challenging grin falters for a second. It was only a few months ago that her and Matt's father, Amber's ex, was sentenced to life in prison—not that he was much of a father, anyway. When Luke moved back to Peak Valley, he stepped in and has even looked into adoption but choose to wait and let the kids decide, but that doesn't mean he doesn't see them as his own.

"Fine." Emily stomps her foot. "But I'm not living with you forever. I want to live in my treehouse."

"I'll think about…" Luke nods with a triumphant smile.

Emily runs off into the kitchen while I take a seat next to Luke. My gaze drifts to the football game playing on the TV. "You've got your hands full with that one."

"Don't I know it," Luke grunts, peering over to where Emily has run to her mom. "Got any idea what's up with the women?"

"No clue. Hazel wouldn't tell me."

"How are things with you and her, still enjoying the whole boyfriend gig?"

"We're good… really good."

"Amber sure likes her," Luke comments, then points to the garage. "Beers in the garage. I don't have anything fancy, just domestic."

"I got him one." Hazel appears out of nowhere, carrying a bottle and hands to me, my chest growing warm.

"Thanks." I smile, taking the beer.

"She's a keeper, but I already told you that." Burns points his beer at Hazel. "Don't screw it up."

"I'm doing my best not to," I say, and Hazel glances back at me with a bright smile.

"Do you think we can get the women to tell us their secret or do we have to wait until dinner?" Burns asks, eyeing the ladies.

"Geez, old man, you take all the fun out of a surprise," Clint mutters, gulping down his beer. "Dawn, can we just tell them already? Burns is going to drive me nuts."

"You're in on it, too?" Burns glares at Clint.

Dawn rolls her eyes. "Dinner's ready, let's get our food and then we will tell everyone why they had to be here."

When Sunday dinner is ready, it becomes a whirlwind of activity. Even with it setup like a buffet on the kitchen island and enough seating at the dining table, it still turns into several minutes of chaos.

"Stop putting food on my plate," Hazel hisses as we get close to the end of the island.

"I need your extra plate space." I heap extra potato salad onto her plate.

"You're a bottomless pit." She laughs but lets me continue to put food on her plate.

"I'm going to need the extra energy," I murmur close to her ear and that adorable blush

I'm coming to love so much is heats her face. "I have plans that will keep you up late into the early morning hours."

Clint and Dawn are the last to fill their plates, and when they come to the table, they don't immediately sit. We were never a family who waits for everyone to get their food before eating. If we did, all the food would be cold. Hazel stops eating and puts her fork down, wiping her mouth with a napkin, and I look around to see Miss Janet and Amber have done the same.

Dawn balances Axel on her hip before setting her food down, then she looks at Clint. He isn't someone you would expect to make announcements but it's clear he is excited about whatever they are about to say.

"Yo, jackwagon, what's going on?" Burns holds his arms out impatiently.

Clint glares at Burns before wrapping an arm around Dawn. "Dawn's pregnant." Seconds tick by before everyone realizes he is done talking. He never was a man of many words.

"I'm only eight weeks pregnant," Dawn adds as we all wish them congratulations.

"Oh, I just realized that will make Axel and the baby Irish twins." Miss Janet claps her hands, and more cheers and congratulations are sent to Clint and Dawn.

"You all are going to be outnumbered by nieces and nephews soon." Maria laughs from where she's sitting next to Miss Janet. The two have chatted most of the night, and I'm grateful for Miss Janet. She's helping Hazel's mom feel welcomed. Hopefully, this can be something Hazel and her mother will attend regularly.

"I don't know about that." Amber laughs. "I'm not planning to have another any time soon."

"I've heard that before…" Miss Janet chimes in when a knock on the door interrupts our dinner. Luke gets up and greets McKnight and for a tense second, I don't think he's going to let him in. McKnight's dad and Luke have a history and recently, McKnight detained Luke. He claimed he was following procedure and Eric defended him, but it still rubbed Luke the wrong way.

"Warren," Maria smiles and stands from the table, "you came!"

"Sorry I'm late." Warren nods around the table. "I can't stay long, but I hope it's okay if I grab a quick bite to eat."

"Help yourself." Amber points to the island.

Warren grabs a plate and fills it up while we all settle back into our food. "Are you able to talk about the case you're working on?" Miss Janet asks Warren when he takes a seat next to his mom.

"I can't get into details. What was released to the public is all I can comment on."

"Is Rightfield's son okay?"

"He's expected to make a full recovery, but he'll be in the hospital for several days. He'll also need long-term outpatient treatment. But ultimately, he's very lucky."

"I can't believe a woman would do such a thing to a child," Maria wonders out loud.

"Neither can I," Warren agrees.

*****

"I'm going to help Amber with the dishes before we leave. Will you let my mom know?" Hazel asks while she spoons leftover potato salad into a Tupperware dish.

"On it." I kiss her forehead and head for the living room where I last saw Maria, but she isn't on the couch. Burns and Miss Janet left a few minutes ago, along with Clint and Dawn. Matt is playing a video game next to Luke with Emily on his lap. "Have you seen Maria?" My heart rate elevates.

"She's on the porch." Luke nods and I see her sitting on the porch swing through the front window. "Don't worry, I've kept an eye on her."

"Thanks." I pat his shoulder and head outside. The autumn air has a bite to it tonight, but Maria looks content, humming on the swing. "Did you have fun tonight?" I ask, taking the empty seat next to Maria.

"I did." She nods, not looking away from the setting sun. "Thank you for inviting me." She pats my knee with her hand. "I've been thinking a lot about your mom lately."

"You have?"

"I know it's been a long time since she passed away, but I've been missing her. I think she's happy, though."

"I hope she is," I murmur.

"I think she's happy knowing you and Hazel found your way to each other. She always wanted our kids to marry and have children so we could be one big happy family. I wanted that too, but I knew it was never going to happen. Not while I was married to Warren Sr."

"Did Mom know how Warren Sr. felt about her?"

"I don't think she spared him much thought. Rusty was all she could see. She loved your dad and he loved her. They were beautiful together." She sighs, turning her brown eyes on me. "I'm sorry he lost his way. You boys deserved better."

"We did okay." I look at the setting sun. I'm starting to understand the devastation my dad experienced. I don't want to imagine never being able to see Hazel ever again, and as fucked up as this may seem, I get why my father turned into a monster after my mom died. You never know how you'll react when life spins your world upside down but understanding and forgiving are two different things.

"Yes, you did." Maria pats my cheek. "All you boys turned into wonderful men. Men your mother would be proud of."

"Thank you, Maria." I lean over and give her a hug.

"For what?"

"For being you, for telling me about my mother, and for Hazel."

"She's quite the woman when she isn't too shy to show you who she really is."

"That she is," I agree, "and more."

"Hey, you two," Hazel walks out onto the porch. "Are you ready to go?"

"Yes." Maria stands. "I know you two are probably anxious to get home. I told you, Hazel," Maria wiggles her eyebrows, "that you-know-*what* is good for you."

"Mom," Hazel hisses, linking her arm around Maria and turning her back on me, but not fast enough for me to catch her cheeks turning the cutest shade of cherry apple red.

Picture Forever

15

~ Hazel ~

I have spent the last three days counting the minutes until I can spend my evenings with Jax. Every time I meet him at his apartment, the electricity crackles around us, making me very aware of how our relationship has shifted. It's hard to doubt him. Jax is surprisingly attentive and curious. He wants to know about my day, look at my sketches or the photos I took, and I'm eager to share it with him. He doesn't hold back either, telling me about recipes he plans to make, wants to try, and his future plans. I wish I knew being with Jax would be this good, because I never would have fought it.

Yesterday he installed the security system in my house, and tonight we are meeting at my place after spending several days at his apartment. I didn't tell him I was leaving work early so I could get started on making us dinner. He's been protective, almost overbearing, with his demands to never go anywhere alone, but being in my house with a security system is perfectly safe, and it isn't like I will be alone for long. He's due home any minute. We've been so wrapped up in the new relationship bubble that we haven't been able to keep our clothes on long enough to go anywhere, but not tonight. Tonight, I want to make him spicy shrimp tacos with my mom's mango salsa recipe as a thank you for being so great and for installing the security system.

I'm just finishing the salsa when I hear a knock on my door. Not expecting anyone but Jax, I throw the salsa into the fridge before running to the door and throwing it open. I'm ready to jump into his arms, only Leo Waugh is standing before me, in his uniform, and his squad car is parked in front of my home.

Panic and nausea knock me back a step "Leo," I squeak, "what are you doing here?"

"Do you mind if I come inside?"

"Um…" Jax's truck pulls into my driveway, and I let out a sigh of relief. Leo turns to see who it is and frowns.

"Is that the guy who found your dog?"

"Yes, that's Jax." I cringe, having forgotten Jax helped me get out of a disastrous date with Leo and his mom by telling them he and his nephew Matt found my fictional dog, named dog.

"What's going on?" Jax asks suspiciously, furrowing his brow as he steps up the porch stairs.

"I'm here to speak with Hazel," Leo says, puffing his chest out. He wasn't that concerned with Jax while we were on a date, but he is now? After it had been weeks since our failed date?

"Anything you need to tell her, you can tell me." Jax sidesteps him, pushing me back a step and wrapping an arm around my waist and kissing my temple.

"I need to speak to Hazel about her brother." Leo cut his gaze to me.

"My brother?" My limbs turn to lead, and my lungs suddenly don't want to work right. "Is he okay?"

"Can we take this inside?"

Jax takes a step back, and I get that out-of-body experience feeling as he leads me toward the living room. A roaring in my ears grows louder until it drowns out the words Leo and Jax are exchanging. Mechanically, I sit, squeezing my hands together. My hands feel cold and numb, and I no longer want to hear what Leo has to say. I want to stay ignorant to whatever he has to say, because I know it isn't good news. Police officers don't show up at your door with good news.

"Officers responded to shots fired at the home of Warren McKnight Sr. When they arrived, Warren McKnight Sr. was found bleeding but still breathing. Paramedics have taken him the to the hospital where he is in critical condition."

"Warren *Sr.*? He was shot?" I sputter, thinking I didn't hear him correctly. Am I so worried about my brother that my brain is tricking me into a different reality?

"Yes, your brother's father." Leo shifts on his feet, looking around at anything but me.

"And my brother? Is he okay?"

"He's at the hospital with your father now. Detective Dennison is lead on the case and has asked me to come and bring you to the hospital."

"But he's okay?"

"He's okay." Leo fidgets. "Are you ready to go?"

"I'll take her to the hospital," Jax says with a chilly calmness in his tone. He squeezes my hand I didn't realize he was holding. My lead-weighted limbs tingle, coming back to life.

My brother is okay.

"Do you know who shot Warren Sr.?" Jax stands from the couch; he's several inches taller than Leo and much more intimidating.

Leo sniffs, tugging on his police belt. "I'm not at liberty to discuss it with you."

"I see." Jax presses his lips together. "Hazel, are you okay to go to the hospital?"

"Yes, I'm okay." I bite my lip. "Warren… He's probably devastated."

"We should hurry and get up there. He's going to need his family."

Nodding, I look at Leo. "Thank you for coming here to tell me." I stand, but Jax stops me from leading Leo out.

"Go get your purse and anything you think you might need. We'll be up there for a while."

Jax lets Leo out the front door while I put away what was supposed to be a special dinner for Jax before grabbing my purse and throwing the strap over my shoulder. Jax is waiting by the door with a tender look on his face that calms the anxiety that has built up since Leo arrived.

My brother is okay.

"Do you want me to call Amber or Dawn?" Jax asks while locking my front door and for a moment, I wonder where he got a key from.

"No, I want to see Warren first."

I don't remember the drive to the hospital. My mind is so wrapped around Warren Sr. being shot that when we enter the hospital waiting room, I'm surprised when I see it filled with police officers and Warren at the center of them. His face is devoid of emotion, slipping on a mask of calmness, but I know my brother. He's on the verge of losing it.

"Hazel, what are you doing here?" Warren asks when he spots Jax and me. Police officers part way, creating a path for me.

"We came to see how you're doing and check on Warren Sr."

"He's in surgery, but the paramedics said he lost a lot of blood." He sounds like a robot, on autopilot. He needs to get out of here, away from all the prying eyes, and take a breath.

"Do we know what happened?"

"Just that a neighbor heard shots fired and when my deputies arrived, they found him lying in the hallway, shot three times." His face twists with rage.

"Warren, I'm so sorry," I whisper, wishing there was something I could do. Something I could say to take away a fraction of the pain he must be feeling right now. "I'm sure he will make a full recovery. The man is too stubborn to die."

Warren nods but doesn't comment, and his men crowd around him again, leaving Jax and me on the fringe. We take a seat and for an hour, we sit in silence, watching Warren bark orders and make calls. Tension fills the room with every passing minute. Deputies roll in and out of the waiting room offering no information on the investigation. Jax got everyone coffee, but Warren didn't touch his. The waiting room thinned out after a while, giving Warren more room to pace while running his hands through his hair, growing more and more frustrated.

A doctor in a surgical gown comes through two swinging doors with his eyes on Warren. I squeeze Jax's hand, tilting my head toward the doctor. Jax sits up straight and we both wait for him to reach my brother.

Warren stops his pacing, the frustration and rage slipping away from his face as he stares emotionlessly at the doctor. The room is so silent, I think time has frozen but then the doctor says the two words that break my brother. "I'm sorry…"

I don't listen after that; I don't need the details. Warren Sr. is dead. Instead, I watch my brother, torn between hugging him or staying still. He doesn't want people to see him vulnerable, and in this moment, he is exposed. He isn't capable of shaking off the badge to be a grieving son; instead, he bottles his feeling up so the public can't see him in his darkest hour.

The doctor is gone, swiftly moving away and through the swinging doors. Warren's deputies crowd around him, giving him their condolence and asking if there is anything they can do. He's going to snap, and I'm powerless do anything for him.

"Jax, he needs to get out of here." I turn to Jax and grip his hand. "Look at *him*. He's going to lose it."

"It's okay, Hazel." Jax runs a hand down the side of head. "He needs you to stay calm right now. I called Eric. He's on his way, but your brother needs you now."

"But Eric and Sarah just had a baby."

"Don't worry about Eric. Worry about your brother; he's going to need *you*. He won't admit it and he will be stubborn to accept your help, but he needs it. Don't take no for an answer."

Biting my thumb, I suck in a shaky breath and stand. My legs feel like dead weight, not wanting to carry me to my destination. It isn't that I don't want to be there for my brother, I do. I just wish I knew how to give him what he needs, but all I can do is give him a hug. I don't ask, I don't even stop and wait for one of his deputies to stop talking. I march over to him and wrap my arms around his waist, laying my check against his chest and squeeze. It takes two heart beats for Warren to relax, and two more for him to wrap his arms around me and return the hug.

I don't know how long we stand there hugging. I shed a couple of tears, not for Warren Sr., but for my brother. When I think Warren is going to pull away, he doesn't but angles his head so he can whisper, "Thank you, Hazy."

Picture Forever

16

~ Jax ~

Warren Sr.'s funeral is tomorrow, the viewing is tonight, and I've been doing everything I can to help with the funeral arrangements, including bringing a suit to the funeral home for Warren Sr. to wear.

McKnight has been a stone wall, uncannily like his father since Eric came to the hospital and convinced him to let Hazel and I handle the details. Hazel is worried about him and when she worries, I worry.

Eric brought him over to Hazel's house last night, drunk and slightly belligerent over Detective Dennison not letting him be part of the investigation into the 'eye for an eye' murderer. Eric learned Warren Sr.'s murderer had used his blood to write the phrase on the wall—a detail that isn't being released to the public and something I haven't shared with Hazel. She's focused on her brother, and I want her focus to be on him and not be full of fear that someone is walking the streets of Peak Valley, hunting down family members who are connected to law enforcement and the justice system.

Knowing there is a crazed murderer on the streets and Hazel being a potential target has set me on edge. I can't leave her side; I don't ever let her go anywhere alone, and even when she's surrounded by people I trust, I can't breathe easily unless she's with me.

Reaching across my cab, I grab the suit and climb out of my truck, ready to get this errand over with and get back to my woman when someone pulls into a parking spot next to me. A young woman with caramel-colored skin gets out of the car and folds her hands over the hood, narrowing her eyes at me. "Jax Colson?"

Tilting my head, I scan her face before my eyes widen and a smile spreads across my face. "Lily James. I thought you went missing."

"I'm back from the dead." She holds her hands up, then quickly covers her mouth and looks around the parking lot. "Sorry, that was a poor choice of words."

I let my head fall back and laugh. I haven't seen Lily James in over ten years, maybe more, yet she hasn't changed one bit. "What the hell are you doing here?"

"I thought I would drop off a peace lily for Warren Sr.'s funeral." She glances over at the funeral home. "Is…"

"Warren isn't here." I hold up the suit I'm carrying. "Him and Hazel are back at the house. I told them I'd drop this off for the viewing."

"Okay, good." Lily nods, then ducks her head into her car and pulls out a plant that must be the peace lily she was talking about. "How's he doing?"

"Between you and me, he's not doing well. Hazel and Eric are taking care of him."

"I'm glad he has Hazel to help him." She looks at the funeral home with concern. "When did he and Eric become friends?"

"That's a recent and a *long* story. Want some company going in?"

"Yes, please." She sighs with relief. "I don't think I'm welcome, but it doesn't feel right not paying my respects, either."

"Why aren't you welcome?"

"You know, the whole going missing and all." She waves a hand as if I should know what that means. "I heard a little rumor."

"And what is that?"

"That you and Hazel Wood are Peak Valley's cutest couple of the year."

"We are a cute couple." I laugh. "I doubt there will ever be a cuter couple again."

"Congratulations." Lily smiles and walks through the door I'm holding open for her. "I'm surprised Warren allowed such a thing to happen."

"Oh, he threw a *major* tantrum; there were a lot of unfriendly words exchanged, but I won him over with my charm."

"Good for you, Jax. I adore Hazel. She was such a sweet girl, too sweet. I always worried someone would take advantage of her. I hope that someone isn't you."

"You sound like McKnight, only nicer," I grumble at her. It is getting old having to explain myself to everyone. I had a past, but that doesn't mean I don't know a good thing when I see it, and Hazel has been the best thing.

"Ha, probably because we were cutest couple of the year once." Lily smiles, but the sadness in her eyes betrays her.

"I'll be sure to tell McKnight you send your condolences." I give her sympathetic smile and nudge her with my elbow.

"I don't think he'll care much for that." She looks teary eyed, and I want to ask her what she means by that, but the funeral home director appears before I can ask, and she's gone once I finish wrapping things up. I wonder if Warren knows his high school flame is back in town.

*****

Hazel is on my left and Maria is on my right while we listen to the pastor say a few words at Warren McKnight Sr.'s graveside service. Maria was surprised to learn her ex-husband was murdered, but more surprised by how everyone walks on eggshells around her.

"I made peace with our failed marriage long ago. Had I stayed with Warren Sr., I would have never met the love of my life. We had a wonderful life together, and I miss him terribly. I wish people wouldn't treat me so weird."

"People are weird when they don't know how to act." I pat her hand while we sit on Hazel's couch, pretending to watch TV . "When people learn I lost my mother at a young age, they never know what to say or how to act."

"I suppose you're right." She sighs, laying a hand over mine. "I wish they would fuss over Warren. I'm worried about him. He isn't eating."

"He needs time to process." I glance over my shoulder, watching Hazel and McKnight go over funeral arrangements.

"I'm glad he has you and Hazel, and Eric and Sarah to help him through this time. He doesn't see me as someone to help and guide him, but as his mother who needs to be cared for."

"He doesn't see you as someone to care for. You're his mom. He loves you, and I'm sure he will appreciate any advice you have to offer."

"Warren stopped listening to my advice a long time ago. Before I got sick. He's a stubborn, independent man who wants to figure things out on his own. There aren't many people he will listen to, but I think you are one of them. Help him through this, Jax. He may not realize it until its almost too late, but he going to need you and Hazel."

I didn't have to tell Hazel what her mother shared with me. Hazel already knew her brother needed her, and it hurt her that he resisted. If he wasn't going to listen to her, he'll have to listen to me, but I planned to wait and have a little chat with him after the funeral.

The funeral was packed with the whole town paying their respects, but there were too many people to attend the graveside service and McKnight asked that it be family only, along with the Peak Valley police force.

It's a cloudy afternoon with a slight breeze and a promise of rain later in the evening. It takes me back to my mother's funeral. I don't remember much, but I remember being at the graveside and not understanding why she was going into the ground. I also remember the pain and sadness I felt, and I wouldn't wish it on anyone. Looking at McKnight, who sits still as a statue, I see my brother Eric by his side, with Ericah bundled up in his arms. My entire family is here to support Hazel and her brother, but also because they have become part of my family.

People wanted to bring McKnight food, but he's buried himself in work so he hasn't been home to accept it. Instead, they brought it over to Hazel's house. We tried to bring it over to him, but he refused, saying he was too busy to eat. Hazel is worried he'll burn out if he keeps pushing himself the way he has and asked if I would talk to him. Eric can't seem to get through him. I don't know if I'll be able to, but for Hazel and Maria, I'll try. Even if it means being on the receiving end of McKnight's temper.

When the graveside service ends, Detective Dennison tells McKnight to go home and not return to the office for a week or he'll be forced to issue a complaint to his superiors. I thought a fight would break out between the two, but McKnight, with the help from Eric, finally agreed and we managed to get him to come over to Hazel's house where Dawn, Amber, Sarah, and Miss Janet helped lay out the food people brought over.

McKnight managed to eat half a plate full before disappearing. "Let me go find him," I tell Eric when he's about to walk out the back door. "Maybe I can get through to him."

"Watch out for his right hook. He packs a punch," Eric says, moving away from the door. "I think he's in the garage."

When I walk into the garage, McKnight's got Hazel's car jacked up and the hood open. "What the hell are you doing?"

"She needs an oil change and a tire rotation."

"And you're doing this now?"

"Seems I've got a lot of time on my hands." He reaches for a rag and throws it over his shoulder.

"Need some help?"

"If I say no, are you still going to help?"

"Yep."

"Then why ask?"

"To annoy you." I roll my shirt sleeves up. "You know, she just took this in for an oil change."

"They didn't do a good job."

"I'll tell my brother you said that."

McKnight leans his hands on the car and drops his head. "*Fuck.*"

"I saw Lily James yesterday."

He swivels his head my way. "You came out here to talk to me about Lily James?"

"It seemed like a good way to take your mind off other shit."

"She brought the peace lily, didn't she?" McKnight looks back down at the car engine.

"She did." I lean into Hazel's car and look around at nothing.

"I saw her sneak out of the funeral," he mutters.

"She seems to think she wouldn't have been welcome."

McKnight doesn't comment but twists the oil cap on Hazel's car.

"What's with her being missing?"

"Can we talk about something else?" McKnight growls, pulling the dip stick and checking the oil.

"What do you want to talk about?"

"Anything else."

"I think I'm in love with Hazel." It wasn't something I planned to talk to him or anyone but Hazel about, though getting him used to the idea of me becoming a permanent fixture in her life will make things go more smoothly.

"*Fuck!*" McKnight pushes away from the car. "What do you mean, *you think*? It should be something you know. Are you seriously trying to piss me off?"

"I *know* I'm in love with her."

"Does she know?"

"No…" I scratch the side of my head. "I don't exactly know how to tell her."

"You just tell her." McKnight screws the oil cap back on.

"Is that how you did it with Lily James, you just blurted it out?" I flash him a smug smile, aimed to rile him up.

McKnight presses his lips together and glares at me. "No, that isn't how I did it."

"Then how'd you tell her?"

"That's between her and I." McKnight sucks in a breath and looks away. "You're not good enough for her, you know."

"I know, but I'm going to do everything in my power to be who she needs."

"I really want to hate you, you know…" McKnight growls, taking the rag on his shoulder and tossing it onto the workbench. "But seeing as she's in love with you too, I guess I'm forced to tolerate you."

"Ahh, big brother, that's the nicest thing you've ever said to me," I say sarcastically. "Do you want to hug it out?"

"Don't ever call me that again," McKnight hisses, slamming the car hood shut. "And we will *never* hug it out."

"Are you going to help me figure out a way to tell her?"

"Yes, but *only* because she's my sister." McKnight rolls his head on his shoulder with a groan. "You should do it soon. We've had too much bad shit happen lately. It'll be nice to hear some good news for once."

"So now I'm good news?"

"You're impossible."

"Someday I really am going to be your brother."

"Fucking hell," McKnight swears and walks off.

17

~ Hazel ~

"She's precious." I smile down at a sleeping Ericah swaddled in a pink blanket on top of a gray, chunky knit blanket tucked in a wicker basket. I snap several photos at different angles. With any other client, I would have been done by now, but I can't stop taking her photo.

"She isn't so precious when she wakes me up three times a night demanding food," Sarah mutters, but smiles.

"I don't envy you there." I laugh putting my camera down. "I do love my sleep."

"I can't believe she's almost a month old." Sarah sighs, picking Ericah up out of the basket. "I still feel like I gave birth yesterday."

"I hear time flies, so cherish it while you can, and I will capture all the moments."

"That sounds like a wonderful plan." Sarah glances at her watch. "I should get home. Eric will send out a search party if I'm out too long."

"Yeah, Jax is on high alert, too." I click off the portrait lights and follow her to the lobby. "Have they any new leads on the case?"

"Nothing so far, and the longer this drags out, the more panicked everyone in Peak Valley will become."

"Between Eric and Detective Dennison, I'm sure they will catch the person responsible." Detective Dennison needed an extra set of eyes on the case that wasn't closely related to Warren Sr. and pulled in Eric to consult. I thought having Eric on the case would be a welcomed relief to Warren, but it only seemed to agitate him more.

He wants to be in control, but he can't, especially not since his father became the latest victim.

Sarah hoists her diaper bag over her shoulder while holding Ericah against the other. "Do you need any help?"

"Can you get the door?"

"Sure." I move to the door, unlock it, and pull it open. "Thanks for coming."

"Thank you for taking pictures. I can't wait to see them." Sarah steps through the door. "I'll see you at Sunday dinner?"

"Yes, and I'm bringing my mom," I say, then frown. "Though I'm not sure if Warren will come."

"He'll come around. He's got a lot on his plate and needs time."

"I hope so," I say, and we wave goodbye. I shut the door and lock it like I promised Jax I would, then I go back into the conference room to put away the photography equipment and props. Business hasn't been that great since Warren's father was killed. Locking my door hasn't exactly prevented walk-ins to occur, but the lack of people on the streets has. Everyone is scared and no one wants to leave their homes.

When I finish tidying up the conference room and head to the lobby desk, my business phone is ringing.

"Hazel Wood Designs."

"Is this Hazel?" a young man asks on the other end.

"Yes, I'm Hazel."

"Do you take senior pictures?"

"I do." I open my calendar app on my laptop. "I have a senior pictures package, which includes a portrait shoot and three location shoots. Is that what you are looking for?"

"I just need one location shoot."

"Okay, and when were you thinking you want to have this done?" It isn't common for the kid to book appointments. At least, during the short period of time I've been open I haven't had one do it themselves, but I'm not one to turn away business.

"Today."

"Today?" I look outside at the deep gray clouds heavy with rain. "I think it's supposed to rain today… Is your location shoot indoors?"

"No, but I need the photos as soon as possible so I can get them in the yearbook. Do you have time today?"

"I can't guarantee the shots will be any good if it starts to rain. Are you sure it has to be today? We could do an indoor shoot or we can do a portrait shoot."

"It needs to be today," he whines, and I'm tempted to ask to speak to his mom. "Please. I really want to have my senior pictures taken at the old barn north of town by the creek."

I bite my lip. "The old barn?" That's a bit out there and with it being late September, the trees would still have the fall leaves, but without any good sunlight, I don't think I can capture the background as well. "I'm not sure the lighting will be good."

"*Please,* Hazel," the boy begs. "I really need them. My mom told me to call you sooner, but I forgot, and she's going to be really mad if I don't get my senior picture in the yearbook. My mom can pay you extra." I'm not sure he should be promising his mom's money to anyone, but I feel for the boy. His mom probably tasked him with scheduling the appointment to teach him responsibility.

"She doesn't need to pay me extra." I sigh. "I can be there in about forty-five minutes, but make sure your mother knows I can't promise these pictures will turn out. The storm clouds will make everything look dark and gloomy."

"That's perfect. I'm dark and gloomy, anyway." The kid chuckles, and I'm not sure he's joking.

"Okay, and what's your name?"

"My name?"

"Yes, your name so I can put you in my system."

"Oh, um… my name's Aaron."

"Nice to meet you, Aaron. Do you have a last name?" His poor mother must have her hands full with him.

"Smith. My name is Aaron Smith."

"Okay, Aaron Smith, I'll meet you in an hour. Will your mom be there?"

"No, she's at work. Is that going to be a problem?"

"No problem, but I do require a credit card on file."

"I have her credit card. Will that work? Or do you need my mom to give it to you?"

"I can take her card."

"Okay," Aaron says and rattles off the credit card information while I log it into my system and book his appointment.

When we hang up, I call Jax, only he doesn't answer, so I leave a voicemail letting him know where I'm going and how long I'll be. I know I shouldn't go out alone, but Aaron sounded like a clueless teenage boy trying to show his mom that he can be responsible. Besides, the suspect they're looking for is a woman, not a teenage boy.

*****

Aaron is already waiting outside his car when I pull up to the old barn thirty minutes north of Peak Valley. He doesn't look dressed for senior pictures in worn jeans, running shoes, and a faded hoodie. Let's hope he brought a nice shirt.

"Are you Aaron?" I get out of the car, pulling my camera bag out with me.

"Yes. You Hazel?"

"I am." I give him a little wave and walk toward him. Moving closer, he doesn't look like a senior. He doesn't even look old enough to drive. If I had to guess, he looks fifteen, maybe sixteen. "Where are you thinking you want the pictures taken?"

Aaron whips his arm up with a gun in his hand and points it at my chest. "You scream and I'll shoot. Go inside the barn."

I stop in my tracks while my heart turns into a battering ram pounding against my rib cage. Staring at the gun, it looks too big to fit in Aaron's hand.

"Move!" He shakes the gun at me. His hand is trembling and for a moment, I think this has to be some kind of joke. "Get in the barn!"

"Why?" I take a step toward the barn, my mind racing, looking for ways to get out of this. My car is unlocked, and my keys are in my pocket, but he's too close. He'd get a shot off before I opened the door. I'd be a sitting duck.

"You'll find out soon enough," he sneers, his face transforming from a teen boy to a terrified teen boy trying to put up a front.

I take another step toward the barn and closer to Aaron. Sweat beads across my forehead and drips down my back. Even with shaky hands, I'm too close for him not to miss, but I can't let him get behind me.

In a moment of clarity, I grip the strap to my camera bag, lifting it so it falls off my shoulder and my arm holds its weight. I take another step and maneuver the bag so it's in my arms, serving as a barrier between the gun and my chest and then I act, throwing it at Aaron's head. He stumbles back, trying to catch the bag while still holding the gun on me. I don't wait to see and take off for the creek and the dense tree line. I make sure to zig and zag as I run. I don't remember where I heard that will make it hard for someone to shoot you, and I don't even know if it's true, but I do it in hopes that Aaron—along with his trembling hand—isn't a good shot.

The gun goes off when I'm a few feet away from the tree line, and I duck but keep running until a searing pain tears through my thigh and I fall inches from what I had hoped would be safety.

18

~ Jax ~

"Why am I here?" I ask Detective Dennison when he leads me through the Peak Valley police station to where the interrogation rooms are. He phoned me earlier, demanding I come in or he'd send a deputy to haul me in if I didn't come immediately, so I dropped what I was doing and came over, yet I'm still in the dark as to why he summoned me.

My phone vibrates in my pocket, and I pull it out to see Hazel's name splashed across the screen. "No phones," Detective Dennison grunts. "I need you to turn it off."

"It's Hazel, it'll only take a minute." My thumb hoovers over my phone screen.

"It'll have to wait. This is more important." Dennison stops before a two-way mirror. I click the ignore button, grumbling under my breath and shoving my phone into my pocket. Through the glass, a woman in hospital scrubs sits cuffed to a metal table, glaring back at me.

"Who's she?"

"I was hoping you could tell me?"

Confused, I look over at Dennison, who's watching me carefully. "I don't know her."

"Her name is Blaine Edwards. Ring any bells?"

"None. What's this got to do with me?"

"She was arrested for trying to finish what she started." Dennison turns his attention back to the mystery woman.

"And what exactly did she start?" I arch a frustrated eyebrow. All this cryptic shit is getting on my nerves. What happened to getting to the point?

"She tried to smoother Judge Rightfield's son while he was asleep in his hospital bed. A nurse walked in and pushed the emergency button before fighting her off. We had to search the whole damn hospital before we cornered her."

"Okay…" I peer through the glass at the woman. She looks to be maybe in her thirties with stringy brown hair and dark, fierce eyes. She could use a couple good meals to put some more weight on her, but nothing about her is familiar. "I still don't understand why this has anything to do with me."

"She refuses to speak to anyone but you." Dennison side-eyes me.

"*Me?* Why?"

"That's what I'd like to know."

"You want me to go in there?" I point at the two-way. "And say what?"

"You don't have to say anything. Just see what she has to say."

"I don't like this." I rub the back of my head. My gut twists with unease; this has to be a trap. Why else would a woman I've never seen before want to speak with me?

"I don't, either."

"*Fuck*," I swear under my breath, combing a hand through my beard. "Let's get this over with." I step toward the interrogation door. *This is a huge mistake*, I think before twisting the handle and stepping across the threshold.

Blaine Edwards sits up in the chair and giggles. "Jax Colson. I'm so *glad* to see you."

"Why?" I growl. My unease excites her, and she bounces in her chair, giggling like she has secret she can't wait to tell. I don't want to know her secret. Her dark eyes match the dark soul that dwells within. I've stared danger in its face, but never evil… not like this.

"Do you know who I am?"

"No." I cross my arms over my chest, not daring to take another step farther. I feel liked a caged animal staring at a predator, and she's the one cuffed to the table.

"That's okay." She giggles and braids her boney fingers before pointing a finger at me. "You will." Then she taps the side of her eye. "Eye for an eye, Jax Colson. *An eye for an eye.*" A cackle so horrific spills out of her mouth and I take a step forward, ready to demand what she means when Dennison wraps a hand around my bicep and pulls me out of the interrogation room and slams the door, her cackle still echoing in my head.

"What did she mean by that?" I demand, shoving Dennison off me and pulling my phone out. "McKnight's been asking Hazel about that. Is Hazel in danger?"

"We don't know." Dennison waves at someone behind me, and I turn to see my brother walk toward us as I dial Hazel's number and put the phone to my ear.

"You don't *know*," I growl over the ringing in my ear.

"As far as we can tell, she's been working alone. We'll send patrol cars out to everyone in your family." Dennison tries to reassure me, but only hearing Hazel's voice is going to reassure me. Ease the giant rock in the pit of my stomach that is telling me my world is about to be flipped upside down.

"Come with me." Eric grips my shoulder and leads be back down the hallway toward the entrance as Hazel's voicemail clicks on.

"*Damn it!*" I shake off Eric's hand and redial Hazel's number. "Answer, damn it!"

"Where is Hazel now?"

"She should be at her office."

"We'll head that way." Eric opens the station door as I get Hazel's voicemail again.

"I'll drive." Eric beeps his truck, and I make a beeline toward it. I'm in his truck getting Hazel's voicemail for a third time when I notice I have one of my own. Clicking on it, I listen as Hazel's sweet voice plays through.

"Hey, I just booked a senior picture appointment. I know it's supposed to storm, but the kid is clueless and needs the pictures now. I'm going to be late getting home. Heading to the old barn by the creek. If you call back, I probably won't answer since I'm almost there."

"She's at the old barn," I tell Eric, clicking out of my voicemail and dialing her number again.

"What's she doing there?"

"Photoshoot."

"I'll call in backup."

Fuck! Her phone goes to voicemail again as the clouds open up and unleash a pounding rain.

19

~ Hazel ~

I never felt pain so white-hot before, and black spots dance before my eyes. Gripping my thigh, sticky warm blood soaks my pants, and I nearly gag, but I can't stop moving. I have to get to safety.

Holding onto a tree, I push forward as another wave of nausea threatens to knock me over. The trees are too far apart. I need to get where it's denser. Harder for Aaron to find me, and harder for him to take a shot. Another gunshot ricochets off a tree to my right and I stumble, losing my balance and falling hard on my knee.

I only give myself a moment, it's all I can afford before scrambling to another tree, sheer will allowing me to push past the pain. My leg is useless and dragging it like dead weight is slowing me down, but still, I push forward on a hop and catch myself against another tree. The creek gurgles ahead, where if memory serves me right, there are several large rocks I can hide behind, but they won't save me. Aaron will find me, but I need to rest and try to stop the bleeding before I'm knocked unconscious.

Another deafening gunshot booms across the sky. I can't tell if it's thunder or gunfire, but I keep pushing forward, my vision starting to blur as big drops of rain pelt my skin.

Again and again, I push forward from one tree to the next. I can barely see through the downpour until I get to a tree and see nothing but fields. Somewhere along my feeble attempt to get to the creek, I got turned around and I'm back at the field with the old barn. My car is on the other side, and while I can't see it, I know it's there—at least a hundred yards away. Aaron nowhere in sight. I can't hear his footsteps through the rain, and there is no guarantee he isn't waiting by the cars for me to emerge.

Cold, wet, and dizzy, I stumble out of the safety of the tree line and look around. Looking back where I came from, I can't see anything, my vision too fuzzy to see well, anyway.

I can make a break for it and try to make it to my car, or I can get lost in the small crop of trees and pray Aaron doesn't find me. My odds aren't good either way, so I go for my car. High risk, but my odds are better.

I make it two limping steps before I fall to the ground, swallowing my cry. Mud slurps through my fingers, soaking into my clothes, making it impossible to pull myself up. I need a tree, anything to help me up from the ground, but I'm surrounded by tall grass and mud. If only the rain would stop. Lightning flashes in the distance and thunder roars over my head seconds later.

Jax. My charming trickster.

He's going to blame himself for this. He'll think he should have protected me better. I got myself into this mess, and I have to get myself out, and that starts by getting up. I want to see his beautiful face one more time. Taste his tender lips, feel his beard tickle my skin, and stare into his eyes that dance with laughter. I want to tell him that none of this was his fault, but mostly, I need him to know I love him.

With inhuman strength, I get to my knees, my right leg throbbing to my heartbeat and shaking uncontrollably. Still, my mind pushes my body to stand on only my left leg, pure adrenaline granting me the strength to limp forward when a gunshot echoes across the field and something hot and terrifying whizzes by the left side of my head. On a cry I fall again, landing hard on my injured leg, forcing all the air from my lungs as pain so incredible tears through me. My cheek rests against the muddy earth and I try to get air into my lungs, only to choke on the cold relentless rain that pounds into my shivering body.

Hands grab at me, pushing me to my back, but I see nothing, hear nothing, only the pounding of my heart as it slows into a lonely tempo and calmness settles over me.

This is my end...

20

~ Jax ~

Beep…
Beep…
Beep…
"Don't wake him."

Ripped from unconsciousness, I jerk awake, blinking my eyes, looking for the only voice that can breathe life into my soul.

"Hazel?" I peer into beautiful brown eyes I feared I'd never see open again.

"Jax," she whispers, tucked into my side. Hazel's doctor told me I couldn't stay, but the nurses didn't say a word when I returned, unable to be away from her. I had to be here, for this exact moment, and I will never forget Hazel returning to me. Forever she will be with me.

"You're awake." I cup her face and rest my forehead against hers. My eyes burn. She hasn't been awake for two days, and for two days I've been a ghost, trapped in a nightmare. I lost a piece of myself when I found her lying in that field, and I knew I would never be the same if she didn't survive. I'm broken and only she can put me back together.

"I'm sorry I went alone," she whispers, her warm breath on my skin thaws my frozen heart. Color beings to reappear in the gloomy world I lived in for the last two days.

"Don't. Please don't apologize."

"Jax…"

I cover her mouth with a finger. "None of this is your fault. Don't for one moment think any of this is your fault. I'm just…" I choke on a lump in my throat. "I'm just happy you're awake. You're awake and you're with me."

"I'm with you," she whispers, delicately tracing my jaw. "I'm here with you, and I love you."

Gingerly, I pull her closer, feeling my numb body come alive again. I find her mouth and kiss her, pouring my heart and soul into it, telling her without words how much I love her. I more than love her; I need her more than I need my life.

I want to deepen our kiss, feel her soft warm body beneath me, but she's only just woken up and reluctantly, I break away, feeling her panting against my face. "I love you so much." I kiss her cheek. "I love you." I kiss her nose. "I will love you until I'm no more." I kiss her mouth one more time.

"I love you." She sighs, relaxing into my chest. I don't want to let her fall back asleep, but I know she needs it. Her body needs it to heal, to be restored to that beautiful, shy woman I feel in love with. So I wait, watching her sleep, listening to the slow beat of her heart.

Beep... beep... beep.

"Jax?" McKnight whispers from the door.

"Hey, come in." I shift Hazel and sit up.

"How's she doing?"

"She woke up."

"She did?" He walks to her bedside, running a hand down the side of her head. "That's good, right?"

"Yeah, really good."

"How are you holding up?"

"I'm good."

"I owe you an apology—"

"You owe me nothing."

"No, I do. I didn't think you would be good enough for her, but I was wrong. You're exactly what she deserves." He shoves his hands into his pocket. "And I know it doesn't mean much now, but you have my blessing."

"You're blessing?"

"You Colsons like to roll out proposals in hospitals."

"I'm not rolling out a proposal in here. I'm doing it right. On one knee in front of everyone. I like it when she blushes."

"She's going to hate it."

"Yeah, but only for a moment." I chuckle.

"Thank you, Jax. For being there for her. For being here."

"I'll always be here for her."

"I know." McKnight nods and then runs a hand down his face. "The kid was taken to county lockup."

"And Blaine?"

"She's going away for a long time."

"And the kid?"

"He's taking a deal."

"A deal?"

"He didn't help her carry out the murders or the attack, but he is willing to testify against her."

"So, he'll walk?"

"He's fifteen… He'll be put away until he's twenty-five."

"Hazel almost died. She was hypothermic and bleeding to death because of that asshole, and he's only getting ten years?" I hiss, trying not to jar Hazel.

"I know it isn't fair. I don't like it any more than you do, but it's out of my hands."

"Why did she do this?"

"Remember the two drug dealers we took down, Silas and Malcolm Edwards? Blaine is Silas' sister. She thought if she took out everyone who was responsible for trying to put him away, she could help him get off."

"And the kid told you this?"

"He confessed that Blaine called him after she was arrested to make sure he knew it was on him or he would have to go back to foster care. He got scared. There was an incident the last time he was in foster care. He didn't want to go back, and Blaine knew it."

"That's bullshit."

"I don't like this either, Jax, but I'm going to make sure he serves every year of his sentence and that he never returns to Peak Valley again."

"If he ever returns, I can't promise I won't end him."

"Don't worry about him. Worry about Hazel. Take care of her. She's going to need you... more than she needs me."

"She needs you," I tell him, looking down at Hazel's sleeping form. "You're a pain in the ass, but you're her family. She needs you."

"You're her family now."

21

~ Hazel ~

No longer is Peak Valley gripped by fear, moving on as if evil never found its way into our charming little town. People once again walk down autumn-decorated streets, laughing and shopping, making it hard to believe six weeks ago Aaron Edwards tried to take me away from Jax and away from this world.

While everyone else returned to normal, it wasn't so easy for me. Every day I'm reminded of how close I came to death due to my limited mobility. Fortunately for me, the bullet didn't hit an artery. Had it, I would have bled out in the field. The bullet caused minor nerve damage, and I was warned that I may have chronic pain and leg weakness for several months, if not for the rest of my life, but I'm still alive. I don't know what would have happened to me if I didn't have Jax by my side, lifting me up, loving me unconditionally, and bringing a smile to my face. It was a slow return to normal… until today. Today, waking in Jax's arms, felt different. Maybe because it's Thanksgiving and I have so much to celebrate and so much to be thankful for. Whatever the reason, I'm grateful for it.

"I'd like to propose a new tradition," Miss Janet says, standing at the end of Clint and Dawn's dining room table. We just sat down, ready to dig into the delicious Thanksgiving feast—mostly prepared by Dawn. "Before we eat, I would like to hear something you are thankful for."

"I like that idea," Linda, Sarah and Amber's mom, chimes in as several of us nod.

My mother holds her hand up. "May I go first?"

Warren glances at me, concern in his eyes. "Go ahead, Maria," Jax says, taking my hand.

"I expect you all know that I was diagnosed with a terrible disease. One that will rob me of the many things I am thankful for," my mom shares, and my nose stings, a lump forming in my throat. "I'm not telling you this because I want pity, but to thank you all. You have welcomed my Warren and Hazel into your family, caring for them when they are in need, being their friend, and showing them unconditional love. I no longer worry what will happen to them when I… well you know, because I know they will have every one of you to remind them how wonderful life is. To love them and care for them when I no longer can."

Silence echoes around us after my mom's confession. Tears blur my vision, flooding my eyes and running down my cheeks. A mixture of sorrow and happiness overwhelms me. Jax's hand cradles my face, pulling me into his side as he wipes away my tears.

"Well, that's a hard one to follow," Burns says, putting a smile on my face.

"Mom," I sniff, pulling from Jax's embrace and hugging her, "I'm so thankful for you and the time we have together."

"I'm thankful for that, too," Warren adds on her other side, rubbing her back.

Jax scoots his chair back and stands, taking my hand and I peer through watery eyes at his gorgeous face, his blue eyes tender. "Hazel, I don't want to tell you that I'm thankful for you… I think you already know that. Instead," he puts his hand inside his pocket, pulling out a small black box and getting down on one knee, "I want to ask you something."

"Finally!" Burns hoots, but I don't take my eyes off Jax.

"Hazel?"

"Yes," I whisper.

Jax opens the black box, revealing an emerald cut diamond. "Will you marry me?"

"Yes." I nod, leaning forward, wrapping my arms around his neck, and kissing his lips, his cheek, then his lips again. Tears stream down my face as he returns the kisses before pulling back and placing the emerald cut ring on my finger.

"Now that is how you propose." Burns claps as everyone wishes us congratulations. "At least one of you did it right."

Thank you

I hope you enjoyed Picture Forever and would appreciate it if you would leave a review. Reviews help readers find my books and keeps me motivated to continue to write.

Acknowledgements

Deepest love and appreciation to my family who support me as I venture down this amazing journey. I love you all so much.

Madelyn you have been a great sounding board, thank you. You are an amazing woman, and I am so very proud of you.

To my husband thank you for your support and encouragement.

Rachael Leissner I'm so lucky to get to work with you. Thank you for everything you do. You are amazing!

The Next Step PR, thank you for promoting my book and providing some much-needed guidance. You ladies are amazing, and I am so happy I was able to work with you all.

Silvia Curry you were a blessing I am so thankful for. You are a genius editor and I look forward to working with you more.

To my readers, thank you for taking the time to read and share my book. I am so grateful to each and every one of you!

Amanda Lee Dixon

About the Author

Amanda Lee Dixon lives in the weather crazed
Midwest with her husband, three teenagers and
two mouthy malamutes. When she isn't working
on the Peak Valley Forever Series, she is
obsessively reading romance and fantasy books or
pen shopping. Her weaknesses are colorful pens,
planners and coffee.

Connection with Amanda:
www.amandaleedixon.com